WE BLEED

ORANGE

& **BLACK**

31 Fun-sized Tales for **Halloween**

Jeff C. Carter

For Mom and Dad. Thank you for moving to New England and letting me be a spooky kid.

CONTENTS

FOREWARD

My original plan for October 2020 was to release my novella 'The Year Without a Halloween', which was inspired by actual freak blizzards (one in 1991, another in 2011). When it became clear to me how much the events of this year would also impact Halloween, I figured the book may not bring much holiday cheer. It is, however, a story about children fighting to save their favorite night, and that's just the kind of spirit we need (you can find an excerpt inside). To that end, I decided to make this collection of 31 stories to light a fire in the pumpkin of every true believer.

Inside this goody bag you will find stories of every size and flavor. Just as a grab bag may hold Laffy Taffy, Bazooka Joe bubble gum, SweeTarts and dark chocolate, this book has tales that are whimsical, humorous, sentimental and terrifying. I hope that you enjoy them all (or at the very least, find nothing comparable to Necco Wafers).

This book is my love letter to Halloween. It channels my yearning, nostalgia and obsession with the greatest festival of all. It is not only a harvest of childhood hopes and fears, but a time for both teenage hedonism and somber adult reflection. It is a twilight mixture of summer glow and winter darkness, when the veil between worlds grows thin.

If you bleed orange and black, as I do, the loss of Halloween may hit you hard. I personally find this time of year to be a bedrock of comfort, self-expression, inspiration and joy. I hope that you can maintain some of your traditions and explore new ones. I have been fascinated to find some version of Halloween reflected in nearly every culture on earth, and I believe that is proof that it can be honored and celebrated no matter where you are and what your circumstances may be.

I remember, growing up in New England, how the October wind would shake the tired trees and fill the air with orange and red leaves. I dashed after them, flailing my arms to capture every little piece of fall (sometimes I still do this). It was delightful, in part, because it was impossible. Autumn never lasts. The wind that strips the trees also brings winter. Yet even winter thaws. Don't forget that Halloween waits on the other side of summer, just beyond the veil.

Happy Halloween,

Jeff C. Carter
Los Angeles, 2020

FAMILY FRIENDLY STORIES

Hey parents! (and scaredy-cats),

There are at least 10 stories in this book that should be pretty safe to share with children. You may find others, but I think that these are the most family friendly.

<u>All Ages</u>
Take One
Halloween on Mars
Inky's Day Out
The Year Without a Halloween

<u>Rated PG</u>
The Dentist
Haunted House 1 Star
Top Ten Tips to Get Your Body Ready
On Moonlit Rails
The Great American Scare-Off
How to Preserve Your Pumpkin

TAKE ONE

A scrap of parchment fluttered on an iron nail in the October chill. Two words had been scrawled in jittery ink.

'Take One'.

"Forget you losers, I'm going!" Bentley broke from the knot of costumed children. He had berated and bullied them into journeying up the long dirt road, but they would go no further. They huddled in the light of a Jack-o'lantern's grin, too scared to climb the steps of the Old Witch House.

Its windows were clouded with dirt and curtained with cobwebs. Tar black scales flaked from its rotting roof. The weather-beaten walls bulged and leaned, defying gravity and time like an ancient stone cairn. Still, Bentley knew it wasn't a 'real' witch house.

It was just old, and old people lived in old houses, grand-mothers and widowers too tired and frail to open the door for every brat in the neighborhood. His smile outshined the pump-kin when he looked on the porch and saw an unsupervised bucket of full-sized candy bars.

He climbed the first step. The plank creaked beneath his feet. The next plank creaked louder. He tested the final step, watching it bow beneath his weight.

The bowl of candy waited, brimming with chocolate de-lights. The parchment waved, beckoning him closer.

He crossed the wooden porch. The echoes of his steps told tales of dark spaces. He ignored them and strode towards his prize.

As the note instructed, he took one. It felt solid in his hand, a feast of chocolate, caramel and nougat. It landed in his sack with a satisfying thump. He leered down at the kids below.

"I wouldn't do that," cautioned the princess.

Bentley snorted and picked up the entire bowl.

"Yeah, c'mon," whined the super-hero. "Leave it and let's go."

"You're just jealous," Bentley sneered. "Jealous little chickens! I'm not gonna share with any of you."

He dumped the entire bowl into his bag. It was completely stuffed, the best haul he'd had in his entire life. He'd be chowing on chocolate for months while those losers dug in their bags for loose smarties and sucked on wax lips.

The porch collapsed, swallowing him whole.

The kids scattered, shrieking all the way down the hill.

The worm-eaten boards knitted themselves back together. The bowl gurgled full with fresh candy bars. The parchment curled like a crooked finger, calling the greedy children.

THE DENTIST

Dr. Olson, DDS, stood on his porch with a plastic pumpkin brimming with treats. Parents were often surprised that he didn't hand out miniature toothbrushes, but he never saw the fun in that. He decorated his lawn, took off his tie and handed out candy like everybody else. He watched a pink princess trudge through the dead leaves with her family. The crunch of her tiny slippers stopped at the edge of his driveway.

"I don't wanna go," she pouted.

He recognized her as Sarah Blaine, one of his newer patients.

The little handy man poking her in the back with the toy drill must have been her brother Lucas. The tallest, a pirate tugging at her tiara with a hook hand, was Jackson.

They chanted in unison, "Sar-ah scare-ah, Sar-ah scare-ah."

Sarah's father knelt down and placed his hands on her thin shoulders. She responded with a gloomy nod and stepped onto the neat white paving stones. Lucas and Jackson ran ahead, racing each other to the front porch.

Dr. Olson leaned over them with a flawless smile. "Wow, cool costumes! A handy man and a pirate?"

Jackson looked up and cringed. The bent silhouette of Dr. Olson, looming in the glare of the porch light, conjured thoughts of the dentist chair. He flipped his eye patch down.

Lucas tried to hold his grip on a fake smile. The stubs of his new front teeth peeked out of his gums.

Sarah slowly climbed the steps.

"Is that little Sarah Blaine I see?"

She hid behind her brothers. They were small and mute, unable to shield her from the memories of the long stabbing needle and shrill screaming drill.

"Here you go!" Dr. Olson filled their bags with generous portions of candy. The bright stream of goodies temporarily erased their fears. When the last piece dropped, they turned as one and dashed down the steps.

"Kids?" Their father chided from the edge of the driveway.

They reluctantly turned back and droned, "Thank you, Dr. Olson."

The children left swinging their bags full of caramels, Dots, Swedish Fish, sour chews, and fist-sized Jaw Breakers. Each candy had been chosen for its superior ability to cling, dissolve enamel, crack teeth and supercharge cavity causing bacteria.

Dr. Olson enjoyed Halloween more than anyone. Soon it would be his turn to put on a mask and wave his hook and drill. The sugary seeds he sowed tonight would become a bountiful harvest of rotten teeth, bleeding gums, tears and terror.

He flashed another gleaming smile and waved, "See you soon!"

HAUNTED HOUSE – 1 STAR

Arts & Entertainment > Performing Arts > Halloween > Haunted Houses

Haunted House at 1306 Summerhill Rd

1 **Reviews**
Add Business Hours
Click here to claim your business

Elizabeth S.
Summerhill, CT
3 friends
261 reviews

My friend and I finally decided to visit the haunted yards and homemade mazes in Heatherwood Hollow. We got there early like we were supposed to, but the lines were crazy! I recommend they start charging $$$ to cut down those wait times. I always buy the VIP fast pass because I hate waiting!

We left the main strip and saw another creepy house around the corner with no wait. I was honestly over it, but my friend Jenni wanted to check it out. I wish we had stayed home!

I will be fair and start with the positives. No wait time - love it. The front door was wide open and we walked right in.

Decorations - It was a cute two-story house with a nice lawn. They had a few pumpkins on the porch and some fake spider webs in the bushes. I assumed it would be just as 'family friendly' inside. I was wrong.

There was nobody there to greet us (this will be a trend for the night). We didn't know where to start, but we heard voices in the living room. It was just a TV, and it wasn't even tuned to a scary movie or fake news report about zombies or anything. A rerun of 'Friends' came on, the one where they all take too long to get ready. They should have at least put on one of the Halloween episodes.

We waited forever for someone to show up or try to scare us. Jenni looked through the family photos and book shelves for clues, like it was an escape room, but I reminded her that this was someone's actual home.

Then we heard a weird noise outside.

We grabbed each other and walked towards it. We didn't know that the haunted attraction started in the backyard (Seriously, a host or even some signs would have been helpful here).

The backyard was filled with shimmering red light. It took us a second to figure out that it was coming from the swimming pool. A dead body floated face down, clouding the water with blood. It was a simple effect, but the body looked real and it set a totally creepy mood. We realized then that this event was NOT family friendly, but that was fine as long as no one jumped out and chased us with chainsaws.

We didn't see anything else interesting back there, so we went inside through another door. We immediately stepped in a puddle of fake blood (if my shoes get stained they can expect a cleaning bill. Also, we could have slipped and fallen. They should at least put up a 'wet floor' sign.)

We followed a set of bloody footprints up the stairs. I felt so bad about tracking blood up their nice white carpet, but they didn't really give us a choice.

At this point, the quiet empty house was really starting to freak us out. I've never been to one of these artsy 'interactive' things before and I thought they did a good job with it, even if they were understaffed.

We went into the master bedroom and found another body on the bed with a pillow over its face. The pillow was pinned there with a kitchen knife. I thought this was super gross, but Jenni pointed out that whatever was underneath the pillow must be worse. It was another example of the low key horror vibe (I'd almost say 'tasteful').

We went back down the hall and found the kids' rooms. The decorations were pink and there were like a dozen unicorn posters. It was way over the top, and a clue that the designers couldn't maintain the subdued creepy atmosphere. Jenni hates spooky children singing nursery rhymes and stuff like that, so she hid behind me and forced me to go in first.

This was another red light area - the lamps and windows were all smeared red. I guess they chose the kitschy Salvation Army junk because they wanted to smother everything in fake blood. The beds, mirrors, floor, toys, everything. We were afraid to go in too far because we didn't want to ruin our clothes.

Jenni pointed out the body parts on the floor. It was tacky, but at least they were clearly adult-sized pieces (violence to children is not cool!) Still, it was really excessive. There were too many chunks and bodies for a home with just one family.

We were about to bail when we heard someone crying. We had finally caught up to the actors! Jenni and I snuck over to check out the scene.

The sound was coming from a half-open door in the hall-way. I think it was the master bathroom. We peeked in and saw some guy in a mask sobbing in front of the sink. He was writing something on the mirror in fake blood. His costume was lame, just jeans and a flannel with goggles and a painter's mask, but I've got to give credit to the actor. He was really laying it on thick, shaking and weeping. His goggles were fogged up too, so he didn't see us.

Jenni pulled me away and we both tip-toed down the stairs. It would have been nice to interact with the guy in the mask (since he was the only actor) but getting out without being spotted was fun. I don't know if that was supposed to be the point, but overall it was somewhat disappointing. All suspense with no pay off. A haunted house is supposed to be scary!

We made it all the way to our car when I realized that I had lost my phone, so we turned around and headed back in.

It was horrible! There was nobody there! We looked everywhere for a 'lost and found' box. I even tried shouting for a manager. I know this is an amateur business, but it is still a business. Was everyone on break at the same time? Terrible customer service!

I went upstairs to find the creep in the mask. He wasn't there either.

We gave up and left. Jenni dropped me off at my place and sent a text to my phone with my address and contact info. I was (and am!) still mad, so I hopped on my computer to leave this review and officially ask them to return my phone. They have no website or contact info. Totally unprofessional.

1 Star!

Edit: I see that guy in the mask heading up my driveway with my phone. I'm glad they're making an effort, but you can't fix a bad first impression. I hope they don't expect me to change my review!

COSTUME DRAMA

It had all started when The Summerhill Source newspaper printed a photo of our hometown hero, astronaut Colonel Jim Stamford, in his childhood Halloween costume. The buck-toothed tyke had dressed up as a spaceman in a silver jumpsuit complete with a salad bowl helmet. The article was clipped and saved in scrap albums, posted on refrigerators and proudly displayed on school bulletin boards across the county. Nobody remembers who got the crazy rumor going, but I was its biggest advocate.

We were hanging out in Lee's basement after school when I carefully laid out my collection of newspapers and photographs.

"Now hear me out," I said, licking my tie-dyed lips. Even for a kid who lived on orange and grape soda, I was more hyper than usual. "Col. Stamford dressed up like an astronaut for Halloween. Then he became an astronaut."

Lee studied the photos and began to fidget, wound up by my own excitement. Hank sighed and looked at the toy box. He'd started smashing action figures lately. My parents said he was no longer welcome at our house.

"Then there's Cal Donnelly, shortstop for the Rockland Raggies," I tapped his photo in the minor league sports page. "Check it out....dressed as a baseball player on Halloween." I handed them an old Polaroid picture of Cal and my big brother posed with pumpkins.

"That's bullshit," Hank said. He'd really gotten into cursing, as well. "He wore his little league uniform because he was too lazy to dress up. That's not a costume."

Lee put his hands on his hips. "Hold on, Hank. There's more pictures here."

"Yes!" I swept the Polaroid aside. "Colin Davies dressed up as an army man for Halloween. Grew up to be a soldier." I pointed at two more pictures for proof.

"His whole family was in the army," Hank said. "And besides, he was dressed up as G.I. Joe. It's not like he ever fought Cobra."

"Yeah but listen," I said. "They all lived around here. They all trick-or-treated on these same streets. Once you start digging, the pattern is obvious. My neighbor Brad went one year as a construction worker. Now he is one. And Dr. Rheinhart? My mom said she used to dress up like a nurse."

Hank clenched his teeth and grunted. "Jesus! Spit it out already!"

"What I heard is," I whispered to draw them closer, "Some house in our neighborhood gives out a kind of wish that turns your costume into your future."

"What a crock!"

"But what if?" Lee blurted out. "I mean, if you could be anything, what would you choose?"

I pointed to the Teenage Mutant Ninja Turtles on my shirt. "Right here! Well, maybe not a turtle."

Lee paced. "Astronaut, baseball player...what about Spider-man? Can you imagine?"

I looked at Hank. "Well?"

He shrugged. "Truck driver, I guess."

Lee asked, "Why would you want to be a truck driver?"

"I don't care what it is so long as it gets me away from here. Come on, let's do something fun." He lifted his black heavy metal shirt to show the bottle rockets stashed in his pocket. Lee and I also saw the bruises, but we didn't say anything.

"Are we gonna melt some smurfs, or what?"

The rumor spread through the basements, tree houses and playgrounds of our town and soon every kid of trick-or-treating age was debating about what to be for Halloween.

Mothers found themselves laboring over princess costumes, fathers cranked out wooden swords on their work benches and the local beauty shop had a run on 'rock star' wigs. It seemed like the last night of October would never come.

By the time it did arrive, I'd had many sleepless nights that I'd spent changing my mind at least once an hour. I reached my final decision on the day of Halloween, but before it was time to go I pulled off my robot costume and changed back into my Power Ranger outfit.

My parents dropped me off at Lee's. I was surprised to see him dressed up as a police officer. He was a good kid, and he generally followed the rules like I did, but he never seemed like the type that would enforce them.

Hank wore his uncle's denim motorcycle vest over an extra-large black hoodie and black gloves. His mirrored sunglasses made it hard for him to see, but we didn't give him a hard time. We were worried that he might be hiding another black eye.

Lee's parents took photos of us before we went out. I did my best karate poses, certain that the newspapers would use them when I became a real Power Ranger.

We hit every house on every block around Col. Stamford's old house, and we weren't the only ones. All of the kids in town were running alongside the streets, flashlights swinging as they hopped fences and raced up driveways. Even some of the teenagers had rejoined the festivities on the chance that the rumor might be true. We weren't competing with anyone, though. We had our own theory.

"It can't be like a magic wand or a prayer," I'd argued. "That would be way too obvious. People would remember. It's got to be something you wouldn't notice, like a special Halloween treat."

Lee had agreed. "People eat almost all their candy after they take off their costume, so that would explain why so few get the wish. Plus, once all the candy is mixed up, nobody knows who gave them what."

It was actually Hank who came up with the best way to boost our chances. "We'll have to eat every piece of candy as soon as we get it."

I loved that idea, and it was pretty awesome for a while. We dove into our bags after each house and stuffed ourselves with crunchy Smarties, gooey Laffy Taffy and crumbly chocolate bars. Two blocks later, our sugar highs had peaked.

Lee looked at his hands. "Do you feel different? I feel tingles...you know?"

Hank opened his chocolate-stained mouth and let out a long trembling sigh. "I think I'm gonna hork."

I karate kicked a tree. It still hurt. "It hasn't happened yet. We've got to push through, guys! Come on!"

We dragged ourselves onward, gnawing giant Tootsie Rolls, grazing on long scrolls of candy dots and hacking up clouds of dust from Pixy Stix. We eventually reached the final house at the farthest edge of our map. All of the other trick-or-treaters had gone home, giggling with their overflowing bags of candy. We lurched up the driveway, empty sacks dangling from our sugar-coated hands.

"This has got to be the place," I belched.

It was a weird narrow house with red brick walls and a dozen different roofs. They were tented like witch hats, spiky crowns, flat fezzes, dunce caps and round bowlers, each with their own lanky chimney. The windows were jumbled up too, stained glass portals that bulged orange and squinted green as they stared from atop the hill.

We hiked through a maze of whispering fountains until we came to the bottom of an iron wreathed porch. We looked at each other, queasy from excess and excitement, and climbed the stairs together.

The dark wood door had a glass panel etched with intricate patterns and a lace curtain that hid what awaited us on the other side. We stood in the glow of a smoke-tinted lantern and checked our costumes to make sure everything was perfect.

Lee knocked on the door.

We heard a distant bemused chuckle, followed by foot-steps.

A towering old man poked his head out. He had brambles of gray hair that wrapped around his face to his woolly beard. His sweater was equally gray and shabby, but underneath it he wore a fancy, if somewhat musty, suit and collared shirt. His dark eyes glittered as he surveyed our costumes.

"It's not over 'til it's over, eh?" He chuckled. "Marvelous! Now you must all tell me about your costumes."

Lee raised his hand. "Um. I'm a policeman, sir."

Hank turned around to show off the patches on his uncle's vest. "Biker dude."

I dropped into my fighting stance. "I'm a Power Ranger; the green one!"

He smiled. "I think we have a few treats left for such...intrepid seekers." He ducked inside. When he returned, he carried a silver tray bearing three popcorn balls.

We each took one. The old man laughed again and closed the door.

The popcorn balls were dense and lumpy. They were definitely homemade, drenched in what I hoped was orange and black food coloring. I slid my plastic mask up and sniffed it.

The door opened again, just a crack, and the old man called out, "Happy Halloween!"

He locked the door behind him and then ambled away.

We tapped our popcorn balls together.

I gave mine a test nibble. Lee took a big bite of his. Hank pulled off his mirrored sunglasses. There was a swollen purple crescent on his cheek, but his eyes were wide with hunger.

Lee turned pale and made a muffled cry through his mouthful of popcorn. I followed his wide eyed stare and saw why.

Hank had pulled a rubber mask and toy knife from his vest. His jaw worked furiously on the popcorn ball as he pulled on the distorted ghost face and lifted his black hood. He slipped out of his vest and untucked the hem of a flowing black robe. His real costume was a psycho slasher.

Looking back, those childhood memories seem so surreal. I'm not sure how much they're colored by what happened later.

Needless to say, there was no magic in those popcorn balls. I certainly never turned into a Power Ranger.

Lee did grow up to be a cop though, which was kind of odd.

And Hank, well, he was in all the newspapers when he grew up.

ALL GALLOWS' EVE

Tom Shearwood cast an imperious glare down at his victim. The chicken walked around him, seeming to chuckle as it pecked for more appetizing worms. As a boy, people had likened both his looks and his character to that of a chicken. He seized the impudent bird under the beak and wrung its filthy neck.

He left it on the stump by the ax. In truth, he could not abide the sight of blood. His shrew wife would have to be the one to behead, scald, pluck and butcher the creature. Soon the bird would become drum sticks, wings, thighs, feet, cutlets, neck, liver and giblets. It was quite extravagant to eat a chicken, instead of harvesting its eggs, but it was the first day of All-hallowtide. Good things were coming Tom's way, and he needed to grow accustomed to such extravagance.

He dressed for work in his long shirt, neck-cloth and frock, saving the best for last. He slowly slipped the black executioner's hood over his face. The sackcloth was coarse and heavy, yet he breathed easier with it on. He took his first calm breath and emerged into the last pale light of October.

Everyone in town knew that he was the hangman, but Tom bore little resemblance to himself when he wore the hood. His wilted body grew taller. His dainty gait became the steady pad of a stalking cougar. Even his frail sunken chest gained a sleek and sinister aspect. As for the hood, it took on a life of its own. Its rough eye holes bored into others, forcing them to blink and look away. Its fabric sifted his reedy voice into a low dry rustle, when he bothered to speak at all. The scarecrow creases and restless shadows were the only expressions his grim station needed.

The sheriff and his turnkeys had started marching the condemned prisoners to the town square. The crowd was already waiting. The somber peals of the church bell made no dent in the chirp of pipes and thrum of tabors, but the mere sight of Tom made the festive on-lookers recoil. He cleaved a path through their ranks straight to the gallows.

The invalids in front were the only ones that did not shy away. They were in desperate need of whatever remedies they could scrounge. The epileptics brought cups to catch fresh blood, the others clutched shears and chisels to cut scraps of skin or cloth from the condemned. Even shavings from the gallows and strands of the hangman's rope were believed to contain some power over life and death.

Tom ascended and took his rightful place above the mob of sickly beggars and self-righteous spectators. The town's former executioner, Johann, had been a headsman of renowned strength and skill with his sword, but he quit the day that they built the gallows. He found death by slow strangulation to be too barbaric. Tom had leapt at the opportunity.

Before then, he had cleaned latrines and collected carcasses, all necessary tasks for which he'd been unjustly shunned. When he became the hangman, that repugnance combined with fear. It was the closest he'd come to anything like respect, and he conspired to get more. Tom was now in charge of all the freshest bodies and the untapped vitality therein. For those desiring remedies of 'corpse medicine', he was the most essential provider in town.

Tonight, on All Hallow's Eve, he would give these rare gifts to wealthy men and women of prestige. This was how Tom would secure their favor and esteem.

The Hallowmas season had made all this possible. The magistrate had commanded the sheriff to empty the jails, so that the condemned might receive last rites before All Souls' Day. This would ensure that the prisoners reached Purgatory in time to receive the special prayers and vigils for the faithful departed. The turnkeys herded a dozen doomed men up to the platform. It was a bountiful harvest, and Tom's hood crinkled like a black-toothed smile.

They strapped the first prisoner into a canvas hanging jacket. Tom placed a coarse loop of rope over the condemned man's head.

"Hello, T-t-tom."

Tom enjoyed these moments of groveling, brief as they were. It was not until he tightened the noose that he recognized the man.

He grunted, "Samuel? That you?"

Samuel smiled. "Y-yes."

Tom had not seen Samuel since the days when they'd been two little ragamuffins chasing pigs. He had found comfort in the other boy's chronic stutter, for it guaranteed him at least one friend. It felt good to have someone try so hard to speak to him, when most only broke their silence to offer Tom ridicule. Now his friend was grown, though it seemed he would never outgrow his trembling tongue.

"T-t-t!" Samuel clenched his jaw, sinking his teeth into his last words. "I have a w-wife! And child-d. Let-t-t...them. B-bury...mmmeeeee...Wh-whole."

Tom looked away.

"Puh!"

Tom reached for the lever. Samuel struggled against the rope.

"Puh!"

The sheriff gave the signal.

"Promise!"

Tom flinched. Samuel had never spoken a word so clearly in his life.

He whispered, "I promise."

Samuel's cramped features unwound with the serenity of one already dead.

Tom drew the bolt and dropped his only friend into Purgatory.

He felt as though his black hood had been torn asunder.

He was exposed to the eyes of the jeering crowd, the sheriff, the clergy, and worst of all, the condemned. These unfortunates had been sentenced to die for things that Tom had once resorted to; picking pockets, housebreaking, stealing food. Their executions proceeded in a blur of kicking legs and purple faces.

Epileptics brawled beneath the gallows for precious drops of blood and any other fluids that had been wrung from the corpses. The turnkeys fought back the invalids while the sheriff cut the dangling bodies down. Tom hauled the dead prisoners onto a cart and joined the lawmen on their retreat behind the walls of the town jail.

Looking back at the invalids scooping handfuls of filthy mud into their mouths made Tom feel better. He was sitting atop a stack of fresh corpses, and he alone had the authority to render them as he pleased. The lawmen bid him an uneasy farewell and left him to his task.

They passed a hunched figure along the way and cringed. The wizened crone was Midwife Blyth, a peasant healer and Tom's accomplice in such matters. She did most of the dirty work in exchange for early access to his supply.

He rumbled, "What cheer, Goody Blyth?"

She rubbed her gnarled hands together and cackled. "Quite a bounty, this is!" She fawned over the corpses as though they were bolts of silk and lace.

She peeled Samuel's mouth open and ran her crooked finger across his teeth. "Would you look at these? Wonderfully white, hard and sound, they are. He surely took no tobacco." She reached into her pouch for a pair of pliers.

"Goody...wait."

She blinked her bulging rheumy eyes at him.

"Never mind," he grunted. "Tell me when it is done."

He turned his back to guard their treasure and avoid the sight of Samuel being reduced to his most valuable pieces. The poor fool was worth more in death than he had ever been in life. Tom considered making a donation to relieve his widow and orphan, and then shook the notion from his hooded head.

Midwife Blyth worked efficiently, but the butchering took hours. Tom winced as he listened to the sticky peeling of skin, crunching of bones and quivering plop of human fat. When it was finally finished he reluctantly turned around.

The old woman had arrayed the medicines in bottles and canvas sacks, with a small pile set aside for herself. There were jars of viscous fat to spread on bandages for gout, fingers to ward off lice, and gallbladders to be dried and mixed with drams of wine for the deaf. Skulls sat grinning, ready to be powdered with treacle or tinctures of alcohol for epilepsy, apoplexy and headaches. Tom was unperturbed by these neat parcels. They were clean and key-cold, no different from the products found in proper apothecaries or those prescribed by respectable physicians.

The blood, however, made him queasy. There were pints upon pints of blood, to be drunk warm, cooked into marmalade, or made into oils for fevers, asthma, palsy, pleurisy, epilepsy, consumption, convulsions, hysteria, distemper, jaundice and joint pains. It could even be painted on doors to protect home and stable from fire, lightning and witches.

He thanked Midwife Blyth and staggered home under the weight of his good fortune. The jars clinked and slopped, but the teeth were the loudest of all. The little pouch chattered with every step.

Tom shuddered as if November was prowling behind him, breathing winter down his neck. Small pale forms flitted through the fog. They were probably the town's children, dressed up like saints for the holiday. It was curious that he did not see the lights of their hollow turnip lanterns, nor hear their traditional songs for soul-cakes.

He reached his house and arranged everything on the table, anticipating which gentleman or lady would be the first to arrive. Captain Spencer, Mr. Robert Boyle and The Worshipful Oswald Croll all had sickly children at home. Robert Cottington, Esq, struggled with failing health of his own. The Widow Nashe, of course, desired youth and beauty, while the Reverend

Horner simply enjoyed the truculent vitality he gained from quaffing fresh blood.

A sharp knock at the door rattled the pouch of teeth.

Tom froze like a thief caught in the act. He forced himself to laugh. This was his house, and he was no petty malefactor. He was, in fact, soon to be a rich and respected member of the town.

He opened the door.

There was nothing to greet but the cold black night.

Another knock shook the sack. Tom shut the door and shivered. He realized that he was still wearing his hangman's hood. It was soaked with chilled sweat and clinging to his face and neck.

He wrenched it off and wiped his forehead.

Another knock tipped the pouch off the edge of the table. Teeth skittered across the floor. A gleaming tooth spun and nudged against his foot. Tom crouched to pick it up.

The entire house lurched.

Tom went down sprawling, with just enough time to glance up as the jars rained down. He squeezed his eyes shut against the shower of shattered glass and brackish human juices.

He lay there soaking in it, too frightened to open his eyes. Something formless and bitter cold poured through his creaking door. He prayed it was the fog. Naked footsteps slapped against the wet flagstones. He prayed it was his wife. A soft chuckle echoed through his house. He prayed it was a masquerading child, or at least one of his insolent chickens.

Raw, bony fingers plucked the tooth from his hand.

Tom shrieked and slid himself under the table. He caught a glimpse of incomplete hands reaching for the fallen packages of organs and bones. He buried his face in the crook of his elbow and listened to tongues lapping up blood and lips slurping splattered fat. Just when he thought he could bear no more, the squelching cacophony trickled to a dry metronome of teeth clicking one by one into the jawbone of a skull.

Reassembled hands dragged Tom out from under the

table and hoisted him up. He looked around at the grisly throng of patchwork corpses. The only feature they shared was the rope-burn around their necks.

They presented him to Samuel.

Tom gibbered, "Puh!"

Samuel's jaw fell open.

Tom pleaded, "Puh!"

Samuel's black tongue flashed. "Purgatory."

* * *

The church bells announced the start of All Saint's Day. Tom's wife shuffled in with a bundle of firewood. She stared at the table in amazement.

It was stacked with bundles, all neatly wrapped in black sackcloth.

THE COLLECTION

More than one item held with affection
is considered by some a collection.
But there is at my core
something hard to ignore;
a heart in its own lonely section.

I am stuck like a bird with one wing,
recognizing your same sad yearning.
You might think you're complete,
with your two hands and feet,
but there's nobody pushing your swing.

Our two hearts together are better,
so with a bone-saw and rib-spreader
we'll make a connection
through this vivisection,
then I'll swear that I never met her.

UNSETTLED

Something shuffled through the dark bedroom towards the little girl. She pulled the covers over her head. She couldn't see what it was, and she didn't want it seeing her either. Cold breath stirred the blanket against her face, slowly creeping inside, invading her last pocket of safety. She shuddered and hugged herself tighter. This had been going on for five nights. She wanted her mommy.

She was about to call out for help when she was interrupted by a slow, creaking moan.

She screamed.

The door crashed open and the lights flipped on. Her father looked around the room in panic.

"What's wrong? You okay?"

The girl pulled the covers down to her chin, unwilling to expose herself to the invisible prowling things.

"...I heard a noise."

Her father's clenched face and shoulders dropped. He sat down on her bed. "Oh cupcake, you had a bad dream."

She shook her head.

"I wasn't asleep. Really I wasn't. I've been too scared."

He sighed and slouched farther, until his back rounded and belly pooched out like the dark bags under his eyes.

"It's okay. Daddy's not going anywhere."

He was really talking about Mommy. She went away five days ago. She was never coming back.

He kissed her on the forehead and fluffed up her pillow.

"Try to get some sleep now, sweetie. I'll leave the hallway light on."

He flicked off her light.

The shadow in the corner clicked its teeth.

The girl gasped and stared at her father with wide eyes. "There! Did you hear it?"

He turned the light back on with a weary smile.

"I heard it." He sat back on her bed. "That was just the house settling. All houses makes little noises now and then. When you go to bed on time, you don't hear them."

"No, not the dish washer or TV. I hear things move through the walls and come out my closet. I feel them breathing on my bed."

He listened to her and nodded. "I believe that you heard and felt all of that, but there's nothing to be afraid of. Here, I want you to try something." He pressed his hand against the wall. "Go ahead, you can touch it."

She reluctantly slipped her skinny arm from under the sheets and reached for the wall. She winced and pulled back her hand. "It's cold!"

"The house gets colder at night, especially this time of year. Do you remember your science homework about things getting hot and cold?"

"The pickle jar?"

"Exactly. Remember how hard it was to open the jar when it was cold?"

"We had to pour hot water on it."

"That's right, the heat made the metal lid get bigger. You could say a house is like a pickle jar."

He knocked on the wall. "It looks solid, but these walls are hollow. The roof is made of lots of little pieces, and the floor is made of boards. All those different things, the metal, the wood, the bricks and glass, they all get a little bigger and smaller as it gets hot or cold. Even the air inside does it, and that makes a tiny breeze that moves the door to your closet," he rustled her covers, "or the sheets on your bed."

He brushed her hair with his hand. "Does that all make sense?"

She nodded.

"Good," He spread an extra blanket over her. "Try to get some sleep." He switched off her light and slouched from the room.

She listened to the floor squeak beneath him as he went down the hall, and the thud of every step down to the TV room.

She listened to the empty walls. She could hear now just how fragile they were, set loosely over planks, which balanced on piles of bricks, all shifting and rattling in a never ending breeze.

She understood that there was no such thing as solid ground.

COPPER NAILS

Maribel crept low through the darkness, hammer tight in her fist. She crouched behind a mailbox as headlights swept by. The rusty front gate wanted to squeal in alarm, but she made it whimper.

"This is ridiculous," she sighed.

She felt like a lunatic skulking about her own damned yard, but her work required the cover of night. She clambered over the tilted sidewalk and withdrew a copper nail from her pocket.

The ancient tree sprawled in its throne of shattered concrete. It was a towering, misshapen eyesore that had loomed over her house forever, twisting, bending, sagging, yet never quite falling down. Its corpulent trunk bulged and spilled over itself in mossy rolls. Its roots had swelled beneath the sidewalk, forcing it to buckle and slide off at haphazard angles. Some of its tendrils had snaked through her fence, swallowing posts and garden statues. Others had slithered beneath the road, leaving cracked and rippled asphalt in their wake.

She placed the nail against the scabrous bark and raised her hammer. A bitter wind stirred the old tree's limbs. It creaked and let out a quiet moan, the same pathetic sound that Mother used to make. She pushed the memory down and swung the hammer.

The nail sank with a satisfying *thunk*. She'd worried that the noise would bring the neighbors to their windows, but the soft copper took its beating without complaint.

Sap oozed between her fingers. She thought it would look like blood, but it was foul and milky, like the pustulent drainage of bed sores. She wiped her hand on her pants and grabbed another nail. She moved as she worked, striking a ring of nails around the bloated trunk.

The tree groaned as she continued towards its roots. For hundreds of years the tree had weathered lightning, hurricanes, ice storms, even the arrival of powerlines. It wouldn't survive this. Maribel had read that the best way to covertly kill a tree was with copper nails. Apparently copper was toxic to plants. She pounded the final nail in deep, where it could fester out of sight and rot the tree from within.

She stretched her aching back and then scooted across the slanted sidewalk. Something crashed into the yard behind her.

She spun around, hammer raised. A dark heap lay motionless atop the overgrown weeds.

"Nicky?"

It was only a branch, she saw, laying in the same spot that Nicholas had landed so many years ago. It was even broken in the same place as his spine.

She retreated to the house and tossed the hammer on a stack of dry wall. There were a million things to do before she could sell the old place, but she could cross that hideous tree off her list.

She slept fitfully, trapped in the rut her bedridden mother had burrowed into the mattress. Dismal dreams came and went, and a queer sensation lingered in her waking moments. She felt like she was being watched, even though there was nothing at her back but a third story window. She wanted to roll over to lay the fear to rest, but her body plainly refused.

She pulled the scratchy covers tight to her chin. Foolish thoughts rustled as she slipped into unconsciousness. *Did the tree expect to see Mother when it looked inside? Would it even know the difference?*

Morning arrived like a rude guest, pointing out the dust and mildew that had yet to be dealt with. Her bagel and coffee went cold as she argued with the loan officer on the phone over payments.

Nicholas called on the other line. She let it ring. She had promised to visit him, and she would, once the house was on the market. There was just so much to do. She wished that her brother could have dealt with Mother and the house, but of course he was in no condition to do anything.

She dumped the coffee in the sink and poured herself some water. It tasted...*wrong.* She spat it out and wiped her mouth with her hand. Her fingers were sticky where the sap had stained her knuckles.

She sniffed her hand and then the glass of water.

"Oh god."

The contractor was there an hour later, true to his word.

"Your water pressure was off, so I snaked a camera up the supply line. You've got a root system growing in your pipes."

"Are you serious? Can that happen?"

"It's pretty common. A big tree like the one out front can send its roots pretty far. Luckily you caught it early before the pipe backed up and flooded you out."

Maribel clapped. "This means you can remove the tree, right?"

The Contractor exhaled. "It's on city property. I can't touch it."

"I called the city. They said there was a five year waiting list to have a tree removed. Five years! Show them how it's messing with the pipes."

"It's messing with *your* pipes, not the public water main. I can dig up the blockage and route a new--"

"No no no...," Maribel pressed her hands over her eyes, "No more digging. No more projects and price quotes and cost overruns. If you want to add another job, take down that damned tree! I got some copper nails, but god knows how long-"

The contractor stepped back. "I'm going to pretend I didn't hear that. That's a 'Heritage Tree', protected by state law. And if there are copper nails in there, you'd better take them out because if someone cuts it down they could hit the nails and get really hurt."

"If you won't do the job I'm afraid I'll have to look for another contractor."

She spent the rest of the afternoon looking for tree services willing to bend the rules, without luck. Nicholas left her a voicemail, but she was too busy to check it.

Dinner that night was a box of stale crackers and a bottle of wine. She ate absentmindedly while she sorted through a mountain of Mother's old mail. There were unopened letters, unpaid bills, and whole sheaves of tax documents. According to the banks and lawyers, they all required immediate attention.

She found a stack of family photos among the mess. There was a family portrait with Mother and Father, standing proudly behind Maribel and Nicholas. Those were good times; when Nicholas could breathe on his own, and Mother and Father were alive.

Next were the crumbling beige pictures. Mom as a young woman, standing in a line of brothers. The house was the same, but the roof had wooden shingles. The old tree wasn't in the photo, but its shadow draped over her family.

Picture after picture, back through the generations, the tree was there. Its branches hid among the misty contours of black and white. Even in the oldest portraits, all but faded with time, the tree splayed like the afterimage of lightning.

She stirred awake and stood, photos sliding from her lap.

The night air prickled on her skin. The front gate squealed. And a tree swing swayed in the breeze, just as it had when she was a girl.

She climbed on and spun, using her tip-toes to push herself round and round, winding herself up like a toy.

The ropes drew tight around her neck but she kept on going. The more she twisted the longer she'd whirl around. The ropes were very tight now. It was getting hard to breath.

Fireflies appeared in the darkness, crowding the lawn like a family reunion. They paired off, gleaming, blinking, watching. There was mommy, and her aunts and cousins, all waiting for her to join them in the family cemetery behind the house.

Maribel picked up her feet to unwind the swing. Rope dug into her neck, cutting off her wind pipe. She clawed and flailed, ripping her hair out in clumps.

She collapsed and tumbled down the sidewalk, rope wrapped around her neck. It was rough and heavy, and when she ripped it loose it dangled from the tree. It was a vine suspended from the upper branches.

She stumbled across the empty lawn. There were no fireflies. Summer was long over. She pushed open the door, hacking and massaging her throat.

Maribel had survived this house, and she would outlive that tree. By the time she was done there wouldn't even be a stump left in the sidewalk.

She wanted to laugh but her throat was raw, so she poured a glass of water and gulped it down.

She sputtered. Blood soaked her shirt and pattered on the kitchen floor. She pried out the thing protruding from her neck.

It was a copper nail.

SPLIT TEST

"Master!" The crooked little man bolted the heavy front door. "Master! Master!" He loped through the sprawling McMansion, leaving a trail of dandruff along the terrazzo floors.

An alabaster hand fluttered beneath a stainless steel coffin lid. Its owner spilled into the gloom like a pale shadow.

The crooked man arrived, breathless and dripping flop-sweat. "Master!"

The vampire's fangs peeked from his cruel frown. "You know I find that word gauche, Engelbert."

Engelbert gulped. "I apologize, Mr. Drexler, but...there is someone at the door!"

The vampire stopped adjusting his cuff links. One spidery brow arched over a flashing red eye. "A vampire hunter?"

"He gave me this!" He held out a business card.

The vampire's nostrils flared. "No trace of garlic...or fear." He narrowed his crimson eyes. 'Vance Harris, Consultant'. Tell me of this Vance Harris."

"He has cool hair!"

"Cool hair?"

"Yes, and a shiny watch!"

"When the sun has set you may bring him into the parlor. I will...take him in there."

* * *

Engelbert slid open the parlor doors. "The CEO of Darkness, Mr. J.S. Drexler, will receive you now."

The vampire sat in a velvet chair framed by Corinthian

columns and voluminous drapes. He matched his extravagant surroundings perfectly, like a prince in a portrait. The hunchbacked thrall looked out of place for obvious reasons, whereas the interloper stood out as sleek and modern, from the top of his manscaped head to the polished tips of his Gucci loafers.

"Sir," Engelbert said with a bow, "may I present Vance Harris?"

Drexler thumbed away on a BlackBerry P.D.A. Without lifting his eyes, he asked, "How do you presume to enlighten me, mortal?"

Vance raised his leather satchel.

Engelbert pointed a loaded crossbow at his back.

The consultant offered a professionally whitened smile and gently opened the satchel. "This is a tablet with my pitch deck. I'm here to help you become the best vampire you can be."

Drexler nodded to the white Italian leather sofa, but did not put away his BlackBerry.

Vance tilted the tablet towards the vampire and began his presentation. "Did you know that ninety-nine percent of vampires don't make it?"

Drexler drew his eyes in a lazy tour of the opulent ceiling, with its crown molding, sponge painting and brass chandelier. "Lucky me."

"Very lucky, in fact. I can see that you're right on the bubble."

"Bubble?"

"Exactly. In life, you were a titan of industry. You had money, power, freedom; everything. Except youth, that is. But of course, a self-made man like you refused to believe that death was inevitable."

Drexler smirked. "Once you stop paying taxes, you realize anything is possible."

"Which is why you must have found a vampire and secured eternal life. It seemed like the ultimate triumph, but I know how that story goes."

"Do you?"

"When you were alive, you burned a lot of midnight oil. Up at dawn, one hundred hour work weeks, and after that? Work hard, play harder. Now where do you spend your days? Shut away from the sun. You may soar through the night like a bat, but you can never stray far from your coffin. That's at least fifty percent of your productivity, lost forever."

Drexler's fingers tightened on the arm of his chair, spilling shreds of velvet to the floor.

"And you must feed, of course. Everybody's gotta eat, but when you do it it's a capital offense! It takes time to get your 'meals', and more time to dispose of them. This is costing you even more time and money.

"Naturally, you got an assistant. Your thrall takes care of the little things, and the dirty things, and before you know it, he takes care of everything. Now you've become totally dependent on an underling. Is that freedom?"

Drexler's attention returned to his BlackBerry. "You are free to wither and rot. I have eternity."

"To do what, exactly? Let's get back to business. I can offer you a way to passively meet your needs and boost your productivity."

Drexler's fangs slid down in anticipation. "You would be my thrall? Is that why you've come here?"

"I can offer you something better. I can help you scale your operation."

"What do you know about procuring humans?"

"It's a waste of time. Humans will procure themselves, because you have a product that sells itself."

"Product?"

"Immortality. Power. Sexual mastery. That's what they want. Let them compete for it. If a thrall isn't cutting it, drain them completely. It's a great way to motivate the others. They'll recruit more thralls and more victims, building a pyramid of slaves with you as their pharaoh."

"And what is in it for you? You want to drink of my blood? Share my power?"

"All I ask is a percentage of the profits. These victims are an untapped fortune in residual income. You can bend them to your will and inherit their estates, or simply take their purses when you bite their necks. This income stream has unlimited earning potential."

Drexler rose with a liquid motion and loomed over Vance. "Why do I need you, when I am the one who has the 'product'?"

Vance's face betrayed no fear, but he did skip ahead several slides in his presentation.

"My books, seminars and executive coaching can teach you special strategies to avoid the most common pitfalls. This is a ground floor opportunity to get plugged into a network of winners. Join my team of 'Vampreneurs' and start living your dream."

Drexler snatched the tablet with a taloned hand. A power point slide showed an ever-growing pyramid of clip art slaves, some pale and bloodless, accompanied by arrows and dollar signs flowing upward.

The vampire hissed. He had known such predatory schemes in life. "How dare you presume to prey upon me, you parasite! Engelbert, destroy him!"

Engelbert's finger hesitated on the trigger. "Unlimited earning potential?"

Vance smiled. "And freedom."

They both turned towards the vampire.

"I warned you," Vance shrugged, "ninety-nine percent of vampires don't make it."

EYE WITNESS

A sudden noise startles me from a disturbing dream of blood. It's the jangling door of the 24 hour diner. A guy pushes through with his shoulder as he rubs his right eye. I blink my bleary eyes and sympathize.

It's late, so late it's early, what my boss calls 'Zero Dark Thirty'. Back on the force we called it 'The Ass Crack of Dawn', the ink black hours when the serious shit went down. I'm almost looking forward to that queasy, neon line on the horizon that drives the dope fiends back into their dens. Almost. That light is also the start of another shift, another day without sleep since I saw the crime scene. Just as well. The boss is relying on me to run down a lot of questions, like 'how many bodies did they finally piece together?' and, more importantly, 'what the fuck is going on?'

The newcomer squints and shields his eyes. The fluorescent lights are harsh and the janitor is using a mop to stir puddles of bleach and vomit. A parade of drunks had stumbled in after last call to soak up their regrets with cheap greasy food. It hadn't worked.

I miss the soft glow of my dashboard and the pine scented solitude of my car. Give me a duct taped vinyl seat and a Gatorade bottle to piss in and I'll work a stakeout for 72 hours. Anything but this revolving door of degenerates, drunks and drug addicts. But, the boss says I have to meet an informant, so I take another sip from the bottomless cup of swill. The trick is to drink just enough to earn my seat without melting through my threadbare esophagus.

The guy is still rubbing his bloodshot eye. Hay fever? No, he's in pain. Must be a scratched cornea, a minuscule nick with the worst pound for pound suffering you can experience. He gets his whole fist into the act like a toddler holding a crayon and starts to moan. This guy is tweaking. Shit. *My guy* is tweaking.

He matches the description of the informant. I suppose I can't blame him for taking a mental vacation after witnessing whatever freaky shit he'd seen. Maybe some of this unleaded coffee will brace him long enough for me to dredge the information from his rotting brain.

He was the only eye witness. The police were offering a reward for tips, news vans were drag racing around the city chasing rumors, but my boss wanted it more. He was offering cash, connects, dope, even hardware to get someone to talk about the massacre.

Something about it had gotten under his skin. If I didn't know better, I'd say my former Captain was scared. Except I did know better. He'd survived two tours in 'Nam, fifteen years walking a beat and seven as the only honest cop in a dirty precinct. Even now, as an independent investigator, he was respected by both sides of the law. The boss doesn't spook. That means he's connected to all this somehow. The situation was personal, and I'm scared of what I might uncover. Would it test my loyalty? Not while I'm drawing breath.

I throw him a nod. He doesn't catch it. I turn to face him. His good eye is shut now, squirting tears as he digs into the other one. That eye is really red...so were his fingers.

I pretend to be a helpful stranger and give him a pat on the side. "Hey buddy, take a load off."

I yank his sleeve down to plant him in a seat and pry his damned hand away from his eye.

"Nooooo!" He shouts and jams his fingers back into his scarlet eye.

So much for my cover. I have to control him before he

ends up in the E.R. I can't afford to lose him to a 5150, a detox or the psych ward. I have one shot to find out what happened at that gristly crime scene.

I slap my handcuffs around one of his bony wrists and crank it up behind his back. I wrestle him for the other one, but he keeps it in his eye. I outmatch him by several weight classes so I lock him in a bear hug, pinning his arms to his sides. He knocks me down like a bowling pin.

His shadow blots out the ceiling and I curl up, expecting a boot to the face. He ignores me and returns to his eye with both hands. A woman screams, the waitress I think, because a pot of coffee smashes beside me and scalds me with muddy liquid. The tweaker's eye collapses and he doesn't even slow down. He claws frantically like a rabid dog trying to get under a door. He screams, impossibly loud, spraying the air with hot spit and fury.

"Get out! Get out get out get ooooooooooout!"

I don't know if it's a warning to us or a plea to something else. The other diners sober up, and dive for cover. Some land on cowering waitresses, others collide with the short order cooks brought out by the noise. I remember the crime scene photos of tangled, blood splattered bodies.

The tweaker has something spindly between his fingers, a glistening rope of pulpy seaweed colored flesh. I think it's his optic nerve, until he drags out three more feet.

"Get! Out!" He throws his whole body into it, folding at the waist and whipping back his head. A dozen feet of strange slick flesh wriggle between his hands, scintillating in the neon of the 24 hour diner sign. Its outer membrane shrivels, shrink-wrapping inward to expose a thorny column of knuckles and vertebrae. They kink up and crack like a whip, slicing through the tendons of his fingers.

The entire mass recoils into the tweaker's skull. An anguished whine of despair escapes his chest. All of his self-mutilation has been in vain. His head droops and he wavers, limp like a waiting marionette.

I gently move my hands to lift myself from the filthy floor. Everyone in the diner is holding their breath. My palms squeak through a puddle of coffee. Shards of glass crunch and plink into each other.

The informant straightens and looks down at me.

"Hello, detective." An oily voice echoes through the diner. "I see you've been looking for me." The tweaker winks his ruined eye. Something inside coils like a centipede.

I answer with my sidearm, sending a full clip through the freak's head and out the plate glass window behind him.

He smiles again, teeth tumbling from his ruined face. "You shall now bear witness." It lifts me off the floor.

I pistol whip him with my empty sidearm. Something in his skull bulges eagerly against the fractures. I switch to my drop point knife and shank him, panic driving my arm like a piston. He welcomes it, pulling me closer.

"It is time to see your boss." The tweaker presses his forehead against mine. My vision blurs as something in his eye socket slithers forth. Into mine.

I startle awake. The janitor pushes his mop past my feet. I yawn and check my reflection in my coffee. I look like shit.

How long have I been up? I look around the diner and squint at the juddering fluorescents. Drunk club kids laugh with each other, mouths full of greasy food. A few homeless people dot the booths, refolding newspapers and warming themselves over bowls of chowder. I never want to see or smell another diner again. All the more reason to finish the job.

The door chimes with a rusty bell. A thick chested man with a tight salt and pepper mustache enters and gives me a nod. I rub my eye and smile.

It's time to see the boss.

THE SILENT PARADE

Andre snapped awake in his uncomfortable hiding spot in the baggage car. The soothing sway and rattle of the Eastern Seaboard commuter rail had stopped. He rubbed his eyes and peeked out a narrow window. This wasn't the end of the line, or even a station. *Had he missed an announcement? Did they break down?*

He tried to stretch but the car was still packed. He picked the most expensive looking suitcase and rummaged until he found an iPad and a designer shirt. There was also a woman's handbag with no wallet, but a careful inspection of the inside pockets turned up a gold watch and a Starbucks card. The shirt was whack, typical whiteboy stuff, but it would help him blend in long enough to get some food and find a pawn shop.

He drew the sharpened screwdriver from his backpack and popped the door latch. A glance revealed no train personnel. He hopped out and left the lifeless train behind.

Andre emerged from the thick oak tree line onto a quiet street. The sounds of traffic usually lead to the center of town, but he heard nothing. There weren't even any golden arches. So this was one of those upper crusty suburbs, where the fast food joints have wooden signs to match everything else. He picked a direction and started walking.

High stone walls and iron gates lined the block, guarding golf course-sized lawns and sprawling old mansions. He didn't see any Bentleys, but bet the garages were full of them.

Heels clicked in the distance. A frumpy older woman, overdressed for the smothering heat, marched up the sidewalk. Another lady, around the same age but in high-end yoga wear, stepped from one of the big-ass houses.

Andre shifted his usual swagger to match their pace. There was more to blending in than the right clothes. Every place had a tempo. Cities were fast, towns were slow. Here, they marched.

He pulled out his phone as he approached. It was easier to breeze past when he kept his eyes down. The two women met and exchanged pecks on each cheek. Damn, he thought that *boujee* shit was just in the movies.

They broke off without a word. The frumpy one turned on her heel and went into the yoga chick's mansion. Maybe they were related. The yoga chick went ahead, oblivious. Andre had never snatched a purse or anything, but he could have.

They turned the corner onto a street that narrowed to a stone bridge. On the horizon Andre could make out the tips of monuments and domes from the capitol's skyline. By the time he saw the huge man in the blue uniform he was already in front of the police station. *Did the yoga chick set him up?* His body tightened, ready to make a break for it.

She stood on her tip toes and lifted her chin. The hulking cop stooped and pressed his mouth to hers. This was no peck on the cheek. It was long and moist, so wet Andre could hear it. They broke suction and turned on their heels. She followed the cop inside without a word.

Andre chuckled. *So that's how they do?*

As he passed an elementary school his stomach growled. He reached for the Starbucks card, rehearsing what line he'd lay on the barista if it ran out of money. The card fell by a sign reminding people to pick up after their dogs. He hadn't seen any dogs. He looked up. No squirrels, no birds. A bead of cold sweat crawled down his spine. He looked at the school.

No kids.

He broke into a trot. He didn't know if this was a school holiday, but it sure as shit wasn't the weekend. No cars, no bikes. *What was going on in this weird ass town?*

He nearly bowled over an old lady with a walker. "Oh shit!

I mean, sorry."

The elderly woman craned her head forward on her drooping neck and parted her wrinkled, red smeared lips. Andre instinctively leaned closer to listen. He caught a gallon of mixed perfume that burned his nose. A bubble of yellow mucus formed in her mouth and burst into a thick string of drool.

He ducked back. She tottered forward, guiding the ooze to his mouth. "'Ey yo, back off!"

Something yanked him by his backpack. A white lady in a pantsuit had snuck up behind him. She reeled him in and pressed their faces together, turning her mouth at the last second to hiss in his ear, "FOLLOW. ME."

She marched off in a straight path without looking back. The old woman stared at Andre, drool dangling from her hairy chin. Her face was blank, but she jerked from side to side like a malfunctioning machine. Andre followed the business lady as he was told, after he had tucked the screwdriver into his sleeve.

When they reached the bridge the business lady hopped over a guard rail, slid down the embankment and disappeared.

Andre whispered, "Fuck this." He could see the blinking lights along the train tracks from here. He didn't hear any trains, but maybe there was time to hop back on the one that brought him here.

Distant movement caught his eye. He witnessed a silent parade of people streaming back and forth into town. They marched across the train tracks, dragging limp passengers like grocery bags. They were inhumanly strong and efficient. It looked like they would have the train picked clean in minutes. *Fuck that*. He climbed down the side of the bridge, scattering rocks and leaves in his wake.

The usual slope of broken glass, fast food wrappers and torn couch cushions had amassed there. It was the first trash Andre had seen all day, and it was oddly comforting. He could always find shelter in places like these. The business lady flagged him over.

She was crouched behind a tangle of thorny vines. He

climbed over a heap of stinky, mud caked clothing to her side. She looked him in the eyes. "Notice anything strange?"

Andre sputtered, "Like the fucking robot zombie face suckers?"

"I call them 'The Legion'. This will all make more sense if you think of them like army ants".

"This is some alien invasion, body snatcher-type shit?"

"In essence. The Legion have evolved to mimic their prey."

"That old lady was trying to eat me?"

"Not yet. She wanted to transfer information. It is called 'trophallaxis', it's an exchange of chemical signals."

"That was *ratchet*. What did she want to know?"

"Ever heard the phrase, 'Take me to your leader'?"

"Hell no, I ain't taking some alien freak to my leader!"

"Exactly."

"You mean that's their dumbass master plan, French kiss everyone until they randomly meet the president?"

She shook her head. "It's more efficient than that. Did you notice how everyone moved in straight lines, along the same paths? They were laying down scent trails."

"Like pheromones?"

"Yes. They've been mapping the entire network of human society, finding the important nodes and secret command structures."

Andre nodded. "Yeah, the rich people, the cops. What about the school?"

She looked away. "Devoured and abandoned. Unnecessary."

Andre kicked a crusty mound of jeans. "Fuck that," He lifted his phone, "we gotta do something."

She grabbed his wrist in her slim hand. "If you trigger the Legion's alarm pheromones, they will swarm until they find us. That's why I pulled you away."

She tugged at the phone. He jerked it back. "We got to call somebody. We're right outside D.C. They've almost won!" The phone slipped through his fingers and tumbled into the bushes.

Blood dripped from her long manicured nails. "Sorry."

"You stupid bitch!" His hand drooped, numb and useless. "What did...?" His voice trembled, suddenly dry.

She picked up a rag and wiped her hands. "I've got a good thing going here. I can't let you expose me."

"You're...one of them!" Andre pulled the shank with his other arm and rammed it into her stomach.

He stared at the bent tip of his screwdriver. His legs wobbled and gave out.

The business woman inspected the hole in her blazer and sighed. "No, I'm not one of them. The Legion are mimicking human biology and behavior, and I am mimicking theirs."

Andre blinked away tears. "Are you going to...eat...me?"

She knelt beside him. "Don't be ridiculous. I don't eat people. I came to your world to follow the Legion. They are my only prey." She gently stroked his face. "This paralysis will wear off shortly..."

Andre relaxed and his head settled into the mat of crusty clothing.

She smiled. "But it will last long enough for me to dissolve your organs."

The corners of her mouth continued to stretch with twitching black barbs that pulsed with milky venom.

EYESHYNE

Glymrwyk peered from the killer's mind, reveling in the grisly tableau. Butchered islands of meat steamed in a crimson sea. Surfaces sharp, surfaces steely and surfaces wet flashed with lurid rainbows. He clapped his intangible paws and squealed, unable to choose which to suckle upon first.

Blood shimmered on the cold concrete, an old familiar flavor. The knife quivered in the killer's fist, glistening like a dollop of caviar.

Be not hasty, child. Let us dally a moment longer.

Glymrwyk remembered the killer as he had once been, a scrawny child, left in a freezing parking lot. Glymrwyk waited inside an oily puddle and watched him shiver, eager to behold his frosted skin kissed with the blue light of dawn. The child endured the bitter night in silence, content to watch ripples of moonlight on the water. At midnight, their dark empty eyes had met.

The child was an outcast, like himself. The other Faeries could not abide Glymrwyk's dark appetites, so they bound him in solid rock and abandoned him upon the earth.

He'd arrived in the city within its first cobblestone. He'd seen its streets spread far and run black with asphalt. He'd witnessed their first glow beneath electric lights. And he'd seen generations of unwanted children dashed upon them. The sewers were clogged with small fragile bones that strobed in the light of subway trains.

Glymrwyk used the urchin as a vessel. He enticed him with visions of power, control and companionship. The boy showed him savory things in return, like the sparkle of a butterfly trapped in a spider's web. The boy was thin as a whip, and in time he was made just as quick and cruel.

The years had passed in a blink. The killer was now in his prime, serving Glymrwyk's most ambitious cravings.

Patience, let the fruit ripen.

The killer obeyed, in spite of the growing risk of capture. Scavengers and vermin gathered, peppering the feast with notes of buzzing carapace and crowblack wing.

Bloodshyne, bladeshyne, flyshyne and crowshyne.

Sweet morsels heaped in a banquet of intoxicating flavors.

Bring yourself low. Move closer, now!

The killer stooped, sending carrion feeders into scintillating motion. He planted his hands in the cold blood and thrust forth his neck. When his lashes tickled the dead girl's cheek, he peeled back his eyelids and waited.

At last the sun recoiled, melting away in orange and purple streaks. The violet light caramelized atop the girl's dead open eye.

Sweet eyeshyne!

Glymrwyk gorged on the gruesome light, filling his incorporeal form to bursting. It had taken years to orchestrate this meal, and it had been well worth it.

He released the killer into the quickening dark.

As promised, a boon. You shall be able to see the faces of your enemies in the mirror.

A simple thing for a faerie, but it would delight the human and enable him to fetch more glistening wonders. Already, hunger scratched at Glymrwyk's belly. How long would the killer be able to provide?

In time he would falter, and then Glymrwyk would turn his pet into a final meal. Perhaps it would be face down in a prison shower, leaking a swirl of red bubbles down a drain. Perhaps it would be in a bathtub storm of sparking blue electricity. Glymrwyk salivated in anticipation of untasted delicacies. He imagined the killer in flames, crashing through a chandelier to shatter against a polished marble floor.

The sunlight drained away and left them in that lonely stretch of twilight that reduced them both to holes in the purple sky. The world was dark and empty, but for now, they were together.

TRUNK OR TREAT

Sharon knelt down and fussed with Dylan's goggles.

"But mom, I want to go OUT!" Her son emphasized each word by stamping his feet. Sharon usually found public displays of sass to be infuriating, but today it was almost adorable. Dylan was dressed in little overalls and painted tangerine yellow like his favorite cartoon character. Still, she hated those insufferable movies.

"We are going to have fun." It was not a suggestion. She dragged him towards the parking lot. Her friend Janet waved, dragging a petulant child of her own.

"Happy Halloween," Janet shouted. "Oh my gosh, Dylan. You look so cute!"

Dylan shared a sour look with Josie, his fellow captive. She looked equally helpless, despite her perfect superhero outfit.

"I think it's over here. It should already be started," Sharon said.

They turned the corner into a narrow parking lot. It looked like a tailgating party for Halloween. Masked grown-ups stood posted at the bumper of each car, handing out candy from their trunks. Costumed kids darted back and forth, spilling cups of popcorn and towing assorted balloon animals. Dylan and Josie, who had been dragging their feet seconds before, looked up at their mothers with pleading puppy dog eyes.

The moms laughed. "Just stay where we can see you."

The kids raced across the blacktop.

"This is nice, isn't it?" Sharon sighed.

She and Janet strolled among the rows of cars. Each trunk

was open and decorated with its own theme, from white sheet ghosts and arching black cats to elaborate sets styled like popular movies and kids' shows.

"I just think this is better than walking through traffic at night, or sending Dylan up to some stranger's house."

Janet stuffed her cheeks with popcorn. "I know, right? Try keeping up with Josie after she's had a pound of sugar. Never again, I swear."

An old Cadillac with a trunk full of dangling rubber bats and spiders was blasting Tim Burton's greatest hits from its speakers. The skeleton mask wearing driver handed them each a ticket. There was going to be a raffle, a vote for best car, a costume contest, and so on. If they were lucky, both the kids and their parents would be going home with goodies.

"Dylan was having a total meltdown this afternoon. He said this was 'fake Halloween'."

Janet grabbed her arm. "One of the other moms in my group actually gave me shit about this, can you believe it? She said 'Trunk or Treat' robs kids of their independence. Hello, who made the costume? Who gets stuck carrying Josie when she's too tired to walk up hill? Independence, my ass."

Sharon took another raffle ticket. "It's not that we don't trust our neighbors or the community or anything. I mean, this is a community event. I think it's even a church thing."

A clown honked the bulb of an old-fashioned horn. He wasn't a clown from one of those dreadful movies, but a proper clown with a curly rainbow wig. "Attention please! We're ready to announce our winners! Children, come on up to the front and bring your parents!"

Dylan and Josie appeared at their sides with candy-stained grins. The women ushered them forward while scrounging in their purses for tickets.

The clown's white gloves hovered in the air for silence. The children were all suddenly still and quiet, save for the restless squeaking of balloon animals.

Sharon felt the owners of the cars lining up close behind

them.

The clown's mouth stretched to the corners of his red greasepaint smile. "Now!"

It was dark.

Sharon brushed popcorn off her face and sat up. The movement made her skull throb.

Someone screamed, "Josie! Where's my Josie?"

Sharon blinked. She was surrounded by wailing parents in an empty parking lot.

AN ATTACK OF CONSCIENCE

Waylon stood in the girl's backyard watching his breath take form and stain the fabric of night. There was no turning back. For three sleepless days he'd trembled in his home, filling the air with prayers and his tub with vomit. He'd banged his head against his mirror and stared into his ice blue eyes, begging the wicked thoughts to stop drilling through his brain. Now he was purged and purified; only the need to kill remained.

He stood on the threshold of Valhalla. All he had to do was carve his unique mark into this girl. Then he could repeat it across his future victims until that mark became his pattern. His pattern would splatter the newspapers with ink and blood until it became a legend. Waylon's deeds would stain human history and his name would howl through eternity.

He crept to her bedroom window, eased it open and crawled inside. The girl's room was washed in shadow, but Waylon had sucked up every detail from the pictures she posted online, from the type of hangers in her closet to the shape of the dent in her pillow. He even knew when she got home from her shift after school. The scent of her room, however, was completely new, and it beckoned like warm silk.

He took a step towards the sleeping girl's bed. The edge of his knife was all that separated their fates. Her death. His immortality. Goosebumps raced up and down Waylon's body as he languidly reached for his knife, fingers curling around the handle with aching slowness, savoring this perfect, irresistible moment.

The sheets flipped aside.

"Hey Waylon!"

A man sat up in the girl's bed.

Waylon clenched, paralyzed by the explosive decompression of his fantasy.

"A-are you a...cop?"

The man laughed and stood up. "Yeah, hands where I can see 'em! Yer busted, see?"

Waylon's ice blue eyes shuddered, trying to absorb everything at once. He knew this guy wasn't her father, but he didn't look like a cop, either. He wore tight clothes, off-brand sneakers, everything meticulously plain, except for his blue nitrile gloves.

"Why were you in her bed?"

"I was waiting for you, Waylon."

The man flicked on the lights. He was tall, rail thin, and very pale. He slouched with his bald head forward. His face, neck and forearms were also hairless, with a sheen of old scars. His bulbous eyes were wide apart with pupils like dull nickels.

"Have a seat, kid."

Waylon collapsed into the pink chair that he knew was behind him. Where was the girl? Had she called this guy?

"How did you know I'd be here?"

The man stuck his hands out and wiggled his long spindly fingers. "I checked your Internet history." He waggled his threadbare eyebrows.

He knelt and pressed his palms together. "Or maybe...I heard your prayers?" He laughed and tickled Waylon's ear. "Just kidding! I'm your conscience, dummy. I'm a figment of your imagination, here to stop you from doing something you'd regret for the rest of your life."

Waylon licked the sweat beading on his upper lip. A hallucination? It was probably the most rational explanation. When was the last time he'd slept? He breathed an unexpected sigh of relief and stood up.

"I'm going home."

The man shoved him back into the chair. His hand felt very real.

"The time to listen to your conscience has passed. You came here to kill this poor girl."

Waylon touched the bruise rising on his chest and sputtered, "But I didn't!" He sounded surprised. "I've never hurt... anyone. Ever." He grinned, delighted by this revelation. "Go ahead. Just try to arrest me or call the cops, you freak." He pushed himself back up from the chair. "I'm totally innocent!"

The gray eyed man sat on the bed and smoothed the covers. "I've seen the photos you keep under your mattress. I admire your interest in war journalism."

Waylon flinched and went to the window. "Stay away from me and my house!"

"I've also watched you at the pet rescue. Such a nice boy, adopting all those bunnies. And kittens. And puppies."

Waylon pulled his head back inside the window and slowly turned. "Who are you?"

"First you have to show me."

"Show you what?"

The gray eyed man tilted his head. "You know."

Waylon pulled the knife from the sheath tucked in his waist and thrust its point towards the bed. "Tell me who you are right now, or else!"

The gray eyed man smiled. "KA-BAR combat knife. Classic!" He hopped off the bed, landing half an inch from the tip of Waylon's blade.

"Allow me to introduce myself. Sydwyk the Sin-eater, at your service." He bowed at the waist.

Waylon instinctively pulled the knife away to avoid contact. "Sin-eater?"

Sydwyk straightened and his eyes went even wider. They were suddenly golden brown, almost topaz. "Wot? He's never heard'a no bloody Sin-eater? Well there's a long and glorious history to it, mate!"

Sydwyk slapped himself on the side of the head. He blinked, and when he reopened his eyes they were gray again. "Never mind all that. The important thing, Waylon, is that I have seen inside your heart. You're a murderer, no matter how clean your little knife may be."

Waylon held the blade close in both hands, like a crucifix. "Just...let me go. Please, I swear I'll be good."

Sydwyk sighed. "You can't stop your urges, Waylon. And you're so green! You left a trail of clues, and...let's face it. You were going to burn out and get yourself killed soon anyway. A flash in the pan, soon to be forgotten."

Waylon staggered. Only the truth could cut so deep. His knife slowly drooped.

Sydwyk snatched the KA-BAR and swiped it across Waylon's chest.

The bottom of his shirt peeled away, exposing his skin to the cold tip of his own knife. "Don't you want to know how it feels, Waylon? All the things you were planning to do to that girl?"

Waylon whimpered, arms frozen to his sides. "What do you want from me?"

Sydwyk's eyes flashed topaz. "Wot do you think, Gov?" He flicked the knife and deftly opened a slit over Waylon's heart.

Waylon stared down in shock as something rancid bubbled up from his wound and seeped out like hot tar.

Sydwyk caught the black discharge on the flat of the blade and then scooped it off, stretching it out until it dangled like molasses. He sucked it all up and shivered with ecstasy.

Waylon clutched his chest. It was clean and dry. The wound, if he'd really seen one, was gone. Even his splitting skull felt whole again, free from a lifetime of pent up dark thoughts.

"Thank you! You...you did it. You really did answer my prayers!"

Sydwyk's eyelids fluttered, one pupil brown, one green. "Your hatred and desire are now mine. Your style of killing," He licked his lips. "I can work with that."

Waylon fell back onto the window sill. "What do you mean?"

"I'll carve your mark for you. It's good to freshen things

up. Keeps the authorities guessing."

"You'll commit…my crimes?"

"Your mark will live on without you. You are free." He plunged the knife deep into Waylon's guts and then stirred.

Waylon gasped and landed in his own steaming viscera.

The rest of the house lights began turning on. The girl trudged down the hall, shrugging off her backpack and jacket.

Waylon tried to warn her. Air hissed from his punctured lungs. The last thing he saw was Sydwyk's eyes as they turned ice blue.

"Time for dessert."

THE ABCS OF A HEALTHY HALLOWEEN

Apple
Bobbing
Contests can
Deliver hours of
Entertainment and
Family friendly party
Games that are absolutely ˙
Hilarious yet still uphold the
Ideals of every proper household's
Jurisprudence regarding the health of
Kith-and-kin in regards to dental hygiene
Like strong and healthy teeth as well as jaw
Muscles while fostering wholesome habits like
Nutritionally sound all-natural foods and activities, as
Opposed to my next door neighbors that clearly possess
Poor moral character and unsupervised children who make
Questionable choices, the worst of which is their All-Hallow's-Eve
Recreation, which inevitably concludes with that foul and undeniably
Satanic practice of running in the streets and begging that they simply call
Trick-or-treating, but that decent folks recognize as the most unholy night of
Ungodly revels performed by degenerates who like to dress up as and then worship
Vampires, devils, demons, werewolves, ghosts, democrats, warlocks and the slutty
Witches, who attempted to corrupt my sweet innocent little boy with all their toxic
Xylitol, corn syrup, partially hydrogenated palm oil, and yellow dye #6 during last
Year's pagan festivities in the dark of night by tempting his pure soul with a filthy
Zagnut.

THE COBRA EFFECT

Sir Malcolm Buckley strode down the center of the cobblestone street while all around him shopkeepers barred their garlic wreathed doors and people hurried through the last thin rays of sunset. He wore a pith helmet and a hunter's loose tweed suit with high black boots. The badge and ribbon around his bulging neck marked him as a member of a lofty Order.

He rapped the pommel of his ceremonial sword on the entrance of the parish assayer's office. A slot rasped open, and a pair of trembling spectacles cautiously peered out.

"Why of course!"

An elderly clerk opened the door and shuffled back as Sir Buckley marched inside.

The clerk bolted the door and hobbled around his desk. "Terrible news, I hear. Another young girl's gone missing."

Sir Buckley's drooping grey mustache twitched in the brush strokes of a wry smile. "I think we all know where she went." He took a black velvet pouch from his tweed jacket and emptied it onto the desk. A pile of sharp teeth skittered across the clerk's ledger.

The clerk divided the fangs into pairs. "These may be small, but they look plenty sharp all the same. I don't know how you accomplish it, Sir Buckley, but I can only pray that you continue. I fear West Suffolk may be overrun."

"Not as long as you have me on the hunt."

The clerk counted out a tall stack of guineas. Sir Buckley scooped them into the pouch and tipped his pith helmet. "Until next week."

A fine carriage pulled in front of the assayer's office. Its lacquer door popped open and a man in a wobbly top hat, Councilman James Primrose, called out. "What timing!" He waved him over. "I predicted we should find you here."

"We?" Sir Buckley leaned over to see past the councilman's top hat, which was always perched precariously atop his head to make him seem taller. He discerned a pale oval face on the bench opposite.

Primrose glanced around the dark street. "Well, do climb in!" His white gloved hand fluttered like a startled dove.

The carriage shifted under Sir Buckley's weight as he squeezed inside.

Primrose locked the door behind him and the coachman urged the horses into action. "May I introduce Mr. Colin Nash, an alderman visiting us from Gloucestershire?"

The beardless man, in a black suit and matching bow tie, extended his kid leather glove. Sir Buckley seized it with great force to take the measure of the man.

"Lovely country. Wonderful for angling and rambling."

Alderman Nash gave him a wan smile. "As you say, Sir Buckley. We are a growing county, but we have been struggling as of late with our own infestation."

Primrose beamed. "Naturally he heard about our program, and so I wanted him to meet our local hero. We shall deliver you to your estate."

Sir Buckley released Nash's thin hand and settled back into the satin cushion. "By the time that we arrive it will be full dark. I could not allow you to continue out in good conscience. It would be my honor to entertain you for the night."

The coachman pulled up directly to the heavy main door as instructed. Sir Buckley went first and unlocked an antechamber. He sounded the all clear and Councilman Primrose and the young alderman disembarked.

The coachman waited until the gentlemen were safe behind an iron gate before dashing off to the fortified carriage house.

Sir Buckley barred the way with a silver crucifix and a

crystal decanter.

"Before I invite you in, I must first perform a necessary test."

Alderman Nash stopped short.

Primrose grinned. "Allow me." He removed his glove and held out his hand.

Sir Buckley dribbled water from the decanter into his hand, where it pooled harmlessly.

"Councilman Primrose, I invite you into my home. Alderman, please present your hand."

"What is it?

"This test uses holy water."

The young man blanched. "This is rather...sacrilegious."

"It is also rather effective. How do you do it in Gloucestershire?"

Nash pulled off his glove. "I have instituted a strict curfew. No business is conducted and no visitors are received after sundown."

Sir Buckley poured the water into his palm to no effect. "Alderman Nash, I cordially invite you into my home. You will find hand towels to your left."

After a tour of the trophy room and a meal of venison, cheese and raisin pudding, they retired to the parlor with cognac to discuss the business in question.

"The vampire problem," Sir Buckley said, "can be resolved with the proper incentives. Though deadly, these creatures are, on the whole, no more terrifying to the average pauper than the prospect of the workhouse or a debtor's prison. Placing a bounty on these bloodthirsty vermin will ensure their eradication by the very same lower classes that they feed upon."

Nash cocked his head. "I understand that you collect these bounties as well."

Sir Buckley touched a match to his cigar and then waved it out. "Unfortunately, it is the only game worth hunting in our civilized country. When I was in India, I was a member of the Maharaja's shooting party. We bagged that lion you see mounted over there, along with six tigers, forty buffaloes, and a bull elephant."

Primrose raised his glass. "West Suffolk is indeed fortunate to count Sir Buckley among her sons. His return from the Indian Civil Service could not have happened at a more opportune time. He alone has accounted for a considerable number of vampire bounties."

Sir Buckley exhaled his first mouthful of smoke. "There was a similar program in Delhi, you know."

The alderman leaned forward. "They have vampires in India?"

"Hmm? Nothing of the sort, unless you are inclined to count the mosquitoes. The real menace there was the cobra! Vicious, spitting creatures as thick as your forearm and longer than you are tall. It wasn't enough to beat the tall grass. One had to mind the shadow of every curb and scout beneath the bench in every garden. They nested in sewers, crawled through pipes, sometimes they fell from the awnings and minarets! The epidemic became so great that the Viceroy declared a bounty of three rupees for every dead cobra."

"And did it work?" Primrose asked.

"Marvelously, at first. Are you familiar with the term 'Jugaad'?"

"I confess I have never heard of it," Nash said. "I suppose it is a Hindi word?"

Sir Buckley smiled around his cigar. "Full marks for the young alderman. Indeed, it is a Hindi colloquialism. Jugaad is a clever workaround, what we would call a 'bodge'."

He stood and gestured for them to do the same.

"If you will follow me, I shall show you a project in the cellar that perfectly demonstrates this concept."

They followed him to a locked door. He opened it with an iron key and stood aside. Primrose peered down at a spiral staircase lined with pulsing gas fed sconces. "I hadn't the faintest notion you had a workshop down there." He stood firm, in no particular hurry to take the first step.

Sir Buckley pulled the door shut behind himself, awkwardly squeezing the others onto the stairs. He locked the door and goaded them downward, filling the winding stairwell with his voice. "The locals turned in scores of slain cobras and collected a windfall of rupees. The architects of the program prided themselves on their cleverness, believing that the cobras would be extinct within a week. Imagine how perplexed they were when the cobra population rebounded, despite the steady trade of corpses for rewards."

They reached the bottom and entered the spacious, vaulted cellar. In place of coal bins there were workbenches, stacks of crates and yards of coiled rubber tubing.

"The locals were turning such a handsome profit that some enterprising chaps had begun to breed their own cobras. You see, that was their *Jugaad*. And this…is mine."

He pulled a filthy sheet off a table, revealing an emaciated cadaver bound in chains.

Alderman Nash gasped.

Primrose covered his mouth with his sleeve. "Good heavens, Buckley! Don't tell me you're making a trophy from one of your slain vampires."

Sir Buckley chortled. "There's a thought! I may as well, for this one has all but dried up."

He wiggled the corpse's toe and its head jerked up.

Primrose yelped and nearly bowled Nash over.

The vampire's hiss was just a leak of dry air. Its jaw had been broken and wired open. Its fangs had been extracted, and rubber tubes had been installed in their empty sockets.

"I returned to West Suffolk the moment I heard about the vampire outbreak," Sir Buckley said. "I knew that the first person to breed them would have a powerful advantage. It took some 'bodging', but I finally cornered the market!"

Alderman Nash smashed a crate to the floor, snatched up a jagged plank and pierced the captive vampire's chest. Its screech echoed off the cellar walls, outliving the quivers of its impaled heart.

Primrose retreated towards the stairs. "Good show, Mr. Nash! We won't let him get away with this!"

Sir Buckley wheeled towards him. "You are the one who brought a vampire to my house!" He lifted a crucifix from the workbench and thrust it in the alderman's face.

Nash's pale face contorted into a skeletal, black eyed grin that sprouted long needle sharp fangs. He hissed, fierce and spitting.

Primrose stuttered, "What in the name of-? Your test! The holy water!"

"That was tap water, a ruse to get you both inside." Sir Buckley picked up a vial. "This is the real item, blessed and consecrated. I assure you, it will burn on contact."

He indicated the table. "Climb aboard, Mr. Nash, or I'll melt you like dregs of pig tallow and toss your limbless body up there myself."

He prodded Nash backwards with the gleaming crucifix.

"That's a good chap." Sir Buckley chortled breathlessly. He used the crucifix to tap a rusty pair of pliers. "Don't worry about your fangs, you won't miss them." Next he tapped the rubber tubing. "I'll keep you well fed with girls from the foul ward."

Primrose gripped the railing and whined. "What madness is this?"

"Nash used you to get to me, but I saw through him immediately. I have witnessed the subtle changes firsthand in the girls I've transfused with the vampire's corrupted blood. Even before they sprout fangs, their skin grows colder. In stillness, they become like marble. In motion they are all glide and ripple. You see it in their eyes most of all. Hard as anthracite, black and glittering."

Sir Buckley shuddered with a delicious thrill from his mustache to his jowls. "I enjoy this trade immensely, Councilman, and I thank you for delivering a new broodmare for my farm."

"By all means catch him, Buckley, but I implore you to let

me go!"

"I brought you down here to feed Mr. Nash, but I will give you something from him in return. I promise to fetch a good price for your fangs when they grow in."

Nash covered his eyes behind one arm and lashed out with the talons on his other hand, blindly swiping for his captor's swollen belly.

Sir Buckley brought the crucifix down on the vampire's skull and dashed him to the ground.

The iron key tumbled through a tear in his coat.

Nash's pale hand shot out and caught the key in midair.

Sir Buckley flung the holy water, but the iron key was already sliding to Primrose's feet.

The councilman clutched the key to his chest. "You're all monsters!" He fled up the stairs and vanished.

"Blast!" Sir Buckley smashed the empty vial on the vampire's smoldering body. "You will pay for that. I'll extract it tenfold from your wretched hide."

Nash's exposed ribs rattled, and his breath came in hitches like laughter. "You never finished…your story."

Sir Buckley slammed him onto the table and cranked a chain across his chest. "The officials discovered the fraud and ended the program. When the market collapsed, the cobra breeders set all of the worthless vermin loose."

He gripped one of Nash's fangs with the pliers. "Did you think I would chase after the councilman and give you a chance to escape?"

He wrenched the tooth, slowly twisting it out to expose its twitching nerves and specialized muscles. "You will never again feel the cool air on your skin while you stalk through the night. You will be force fed the diseased blood of whores through a tube."

He ripped out the other fang. "You will watch as I butcher your progeny in front of you!"

Nash burbled, spattering his lips with blood. "Did you think you were the… only one? Primrose shall expose you."

His jaw hung loose in a serpent's mirthless grin. "Once we are worthless...we shall be expelled from the barns and basements. We will flood the streets of your city and...swallow it whole."

Buckley staggered back with revelation. "*Jugaad.*"

HALLOWEEN ON MARS

The sky is turning red and the sun is growing dim. It's almost time for the Martian colony to celebrate Halloween! Do you know the origins of this spooky holiday?

What is Halloween?

Halloween is a mix of ancient harvest festivals that honor our deceased ancestors and frighten away evil spirits.

When is Halloween?

Halloween on Earth is calibrated to the cold, dark mid-point of its Autumnal Equinox and Southern Solstice. That doesn't make a lot of sense for Mars' **Darian Calendar**. With our irregular orbit and 24 months, Earth Halloween can come more than twice a year!

Here on Mars, the most dramatic dimming of the Sun comes not during winter (aphelion), but in the month of **Simha**, when the planet is closest to the Sun (approx. Ls = 260°). The rising temperatures mark the beginning of **Dust Storm Season**.

This was a very frightening time in the early days of the Colony. Scattered electrostatic dust would cover the solar cells and clog vital machinery. Raging storms blotted out the sun, plunging Mars into darkness for months, sometimes years.

We have since adapted and made great progress in our new home, but Simha is still an eerie and dangerous time. The increased solar radiation stirs up millions of dust devils, up to fifty times as wide and ten times as high as those on Earth. These mischievous whirlwinds are unpredictable, creating electrical fields that interfere with equipment or appearing out of nowhere to sweep things clean.

Since the early days, many explorers have been lost in *redouts*[1]. Terraforming has thickened our atmosphere, and this has produced more powerful gusts of wind. Anyone venturing across the surface unprotected might be injured by flying debris, knocked into a canyon or buried alive in a sand drift[2].

Even those sealed safely inside can feel fear. When the wind moans over the air locks of the subterranean zones and blood red shapes dance in the mist, scratching at the Domes, it's enough to chill the spines of the bravest colonists.

This is why Martians celebrate Halloween for all 27 days of Simha.

How do people celebrate?

Honoring the spirits of our ancestors grew more complicated once we became a multi-planet species. While modern Martians are **upcycled** after death, the early Colonists had to leave the remains of their ancestors on Earth. This is why some older Martians create family altars in the center of the Domes.

Religious observances tied to Earth's moon, Luna, have been adapted[3] to the Darian Calendar.

Traditionally, adults set out offerings of food and candy. Nowadays, most kids send their drones to trick-or-treat for them while they attend Halloween parties. Costumes and disguises are worn to the carnivals in the large sealed habitats. These avatars appear only in other people's **Augmented Reality** lenses, so your imagination is the limit! Perhaps you'll appear as a Space Pirate, a 21st century Death Cultist or a Late Stage Capitalist. Spooky!

Another popular Halloween activity is using the **Ouija Net**. Conjure up simulacra of the dead to answer your questions! Remember to be polite. One day there will be a simulacrum of you.

Perhaps the most enduring symbol of Halloween is the Jack-O'-lantern. For this traditional activity, you will first need a *Tumblepumpkin*[4].

How to Carve a Tumblepumpkin

Step 1: Remove the spines from your Tumblepumpkin. Ask a droid or adult for help.

Step 2: Cut out a lid. Carve the top off at a 45 degree inward angle. Add a notch to help line it up when you're ready to replace it.

Step 3: Scoop out the insides. Clean out the Tumblepumpkin until no pulp or seeds remain. (Do not roast Tumblepumpkin seeds! They are highly toxic!)

Step 4: Carve your design. Invent your own or choose from the traditional patterns like helmeted explorer, famous astrophysicist or Emperor Musk.

Step 5: Light your pumpkin. Insert a solar diode to make your creation shine!

Step 6: Place your pumpkin. Set your pumpkin on your doorstep to welcome visitors and scare away spooks.

Step 7: Monitor your pumpkin carefully for signs of **Crispr Thrips** infestation [5]. If your pumpkin becomes bioluminescent or begins to pulsate <u>alert Biohazard Control immediately</u>!

Happy Halloween!

[1] A red-out is a weather condition in which airborne red dust diffuses the light and erases the landscape and horizon. Low visibility and contrast can cause people to become disoriented and lost.

[2] Every child knows the nursery rhyme about Red Peter:

> *One dusty rusty morning, when scarlet was the weather,*
>
> *I went to see the old man, minding all the tethers.*
>
> *He spoke of the empty Dome, said that we could be alone,*
>
> *then pushed me down one big dune,*
>
> *red sand shushed my screaming soon.*
>
> *I'll stay for Red Peter forever*

[3] We cannot synchronize lunar holidays with our moons because Phobos is too speedy and Deimos is too distant, so we continue to rely on Earth's moon Luna.

The **Obon festival/Ghost Festival** is held during the 7th month of the lunar calendar, which may occur here up to 3 times a year. For this reason, every 7th month is celebrated differently. In the first, a large feast is held to provide comfort for hungry ghosts. If there are three in a year, the second is a solemn affair for burning incense to venerate ancestors. The final festival ends with a release of sky lanterns into the giant dust devils in order to guide the spirits back to the afterlife.

The Hindu population observes **Sarvapitri Amavasya** (all ancestors' new moon day) because it is held irrespective of the lunar day that their relatives died. Because this also happens more than once during the Martian year, Hindus perform their oblations concurrently with those on Earth.

[4] After the **Great Sowing**, GMO plants emerged that were adapted to the harsh and changing environment. One of the most unusual plants to crop up was the **Pumpkin Cactus**. This round orange cactoid has sharp spines that conserve water and protect it from herbivores. Its blossoms can be harvested to make delicious pumpkin spice lattes, but be careful not to tear your environmental suit!

When a Pumpkin Cactus matures it separates from its root system and becomes a Tumblepumpkin. The fierce winds of Simha send stampedes of Tumblepumpkins across the surface of Mars to smash into ravines and disperse their seeds.

[5] Failure to contain a Crispr Thrips infestation will result in the annihilation of your dome.

THE DOG WALKER

When the sun goes down it is time to bring out the dog. I could say that I walk it, but in truth, it's walking me. It wanders from block to block, dipping its nose along the ground like a dowsing rod, veering to align itself along some invisible meridian. We never walk the same path twice. This is somehow both stimulating and relaxing, a sublime state I thought I'd lost when I quit smoking cigarettes. With my feet compelled and my mind untethered to anything but the dog, I am free to ponder old quandaries like, 'Why do bad things happen to good people?' The dog wanders, and I wonder. If there is a larger plan, the dog isn't sharing it with me.

Some blocks make for less-than-pleasant strolling. Broken bottles and soiled condoms sprout like weeds. Shit-stained newspapers and dirty needles clog the gutters. Things shift inside parked cars with dark eyes, human and animal, that stare through greasy fogged windows.

The dog follows a smell to a darkly blotted mattress. It traces the filth with its fist-sized nose and then pulls me onward. We leave Skid Row for a more respectable neighborhood. It is funny how such different worlds can exist right next to each other, completely separated by unmarked borders, unbuilt walls and unspoken prejudices.

Here the people sleep safe and snug inside well-appointed homes. The houses are clean, but not where it counts. I'm no angel, yet I see darkness behind these white picket fences. Have you ever spotted a wife with a black eye, or a child with a cigarette burn? Would you say anything if you did? Of course not, you don't poke your nose into other people's business. You follow the rules, because you're a good person. But bad things happen to good people.

The dog tugs from the orderly cones of street light into the chaotic shadows of wooded yards. It scours the wet grass, nose twitching to discard the earthy night smells from the lingering trail of its prey.

The families here insulate their children from the world with thick hedges and manicured lawns. Do they know how many sex offenders live in their neighborhood? How about yours? No one has ever knocked on your door and declared themselves, like you think they're supposed to, but they're all posted on a government website. I would call it eye-opening, but then, you haven't looked. Like the people here, you refuse to smell the stench of corruption that lingers around you.

The hound moves with purpose now, hot on the trail. I step over a newspaper left to molder in a plastic shroud. You skim the news, glossing over the deaths of faceless strangers. You just want headlines, like that story about the serial killer brought to justice. I know a thing or two about serial killers. The FBI estimates that there are as many as two thousand serial killers operating under the radar. The police may suspect that one is stalking your area even now, but they won't reveal it. They don't want to alert the killer, or he'll change his pattern. Your trusty news helps cover it up. They want the bigger, juicier story. Like you, they just want headlines.

The dog brings me, at last, to a gated driveway. The lawn on the other side is crammed with exotic cars and statues in such excess that it looks like a royal junkyard. It takes me a moment to recognize that the stack of glass and steel cubes is the actual house and not a piece of modern art. It shines in the moonlight, flawless and kitchen clean, but a foul scent has the hound drooling.

It takes off without me and squeezes between the bars. I dig my heels in and hold tight. The beast strains at the leash, eager to be rid of me, choking itself in excitement. It takes me a moment to squeeze through the gate myself. The motion detectors are dormant as we climb the marble steps. The dog claws at the front door, bristling and snorting. The alarms are silent.

Together, we collapse and shift through wood, brick and reinforced steel to breach the sinner's lair.

A balding sixty year old man, caught halfway between his refrigerator and a laptop on the dining room table sees us as we coagulate from empty space. The beast crouches to attack. What trail of evil deeds has brought us to this man's door; what is on that glowing screen? Is he a corporate raider, a money launderer, or another milquetoast weakling who waits until his family is asleep to troll the internet for child pornography?

The little man turns to flee. I let the leash slip from my hand.

The hellhound shivers off its illusion and explodes into a roiling black cloud. The man is engulfed in an orange-streaked void of gnashing iron teeth forged from its hellfire engine core. It devours him with brutal efficiency, sundering his body to excavate his diseased soul.

I catch a glimpse of it beneath the veils of fatty tissue and cascades of blood. It shimmers, brilliant and opalescent; the divine spark of an uncorrupted soul.

This man is innocent.

I call off the hellhound. This is no easy task, but it is the one assigned to me. Like I said, I'm no angel, but I am endowed with enough power to bring the demon to heel. I shout the ineffable commands and wrestle with the snarling vortex.

The void excretes a pile of shredded, steaming meat that splatters across the marble foyer. The mess quivers and contracts into a mewling newborn the size of a man. He flops like a hooked fish as his body ages sixty years. His eyes roll and flutter, scorched with visions of Hell. His mind is desecrated, but his soul is clear.

The hound has already forgotten its victim. It sniffs around the house, seeking the old scent that had drawn it here. The beast weaves a new trail from threadbare odors and licks its chops, eager to resume the hunt.

As we slip through the wall, I look back at the naked convulsing man. Why do bad things happen to good people? I think it is because you invite it. Not with malice, but with sloth. You turn a blind eye to suffering and wallow in the reek of sin. You believe that you can perfume the air with self-righteous thoughts and prayers, but the scent of evil lingers.

And it may just bring us to your door.

IN TERROREM

Martin parked across from the estate and walked along its ivy cloaked walls. He announced himself at the intercom and then studied the intricate castings on the wrought iron gate. The metal bands radiated and crossed in a bewildering design, spiraling off in scatter-shot whirls wherever a pattern threatened to emerge. He wondered if it had once stood as a banner of heraldry that had been stripped with each passing generation. Martin smiled as it parted to admit him. Sure, he could have driven inside and parked by the fountain, but marching inside brought the satisfaction of entering a conquered castle.

The matriarch was dead, but the war was just beginning. Martin was not here to claim her lands and fortune. He was the executor of her last will and testament. Aging oligarchs and paranoid plutocrats held him in high regard for his ability to settle disputed estates. Untangling the skeins of tax codes and probate law was not some bloodless chore of accounting. Martin considered a contested will to be just that, a contest of wills.

He strolled down the garden path, past dizzying hedge mazes and a museum's worth of statuary. Even if he had not reviewed the estate's holdings, his surroundings informed him that this would be a fierce fight. His opponents often had elite educations, political connections and armies of vicious lawyers. Martin's payment came out of the estate, however. The longer the beneficiaries dragged out their grueling battles, the less they received. He swung his briefcase and almost whistled a jaunty tune, before remembering that this was supposed to be a solemn affair.

A white haired, gray eyed servant in a black coat and bow

tie met him at the door.

"Is there an office I can set up in?"

The servant performed a curt bow and led him into a labyrinth of oak paneled hallways. Soot stained portraits of glowering ancestors swallowed the sunlight. Martin followed the butler's starched collar through the gloom, unsure if he'd be able to find his way back without it.

They arrived at a pitch black cavern. The servant flipped a switch and a crystal chandelier illuminated the center of a cluttered office. Martin made his way around a titanic mahogany desk and plopped down in a high backed chair that belonged in a throne room. He opened his briefcase and spread out his files. It seemed that he was to be kept waiting.

Normally the family members were already present and jostling for position. It didn't matter whether they were wellbred or nouveau riche, they all became pigs squealing at the trough. Martin had seen so many patricians stab each other in the back that he could have bathed in blue blood.

Today, there was just a single heir. This should have made the proceedings fairly straightforward, but Martin had been chosen for good reason. The matriarch had left behind what was colloquially known as a 'Mystic Will', a legal testament that is sealed until death.

A young woman walked in with her head hung low. "I'm here for grandma's will." She didn't meet his eyes, but the rich rarely did. It was an affect of the aristocracy, but it may have been due to the cell phone in her hands. She was tall and thin, all shine and bone structure. She wore a tasteful black silk dress, though Martin couldn't tell if it was funereal or haute couture.

"Hello, my name is Martin. I'm so sorry for your loss."

She made a faint noise of feigned gratitude.

"I am now going to unseal the will." He searched the desk for a letter opener and then pulled open a drawer. He found a slim dagger encrusted with jewels that had probably come with the chair. He slit open the yellowed envelope and removed the document.

He scanned ahead for legal terms. "It states here that she had prepared an 'Irrevocable Gift' trust, bound by an '*in terrorem*' clause."

The girl finally stopped tapping on her phone and looked up, confused.

"What?"

Martin squelched a smile. This girl didn't look like much, yet she was the sole remaining heir to an incomprehensibly vast fortune. It was possible that she had outmaneuvered all of her relatives, or that her parents had shrewdly cleared them out of her way, but in the end the matriarch had cornered her from the grave.

"An irrevocable trust cannot be modified, amended or revoked. The added 'in terrorem' clause means that if you challenge the will, in any way, you will lose your entire inheritance."

She dropped her phone and put her face in her hands.

Martin wondered if she would throw a tantrum or crumple in tears. She did her best to keep a stiff upper lip. He continued with the letter, hoping to find some spiteful words that might pour salt in old wounds. He had delivered many a posthumous screed over his career, and considered himself a connoisseur of pent-up blistering bile.

"I do hereby order and appoint my grand-daughter, Diana, the dominion over and obeisance of our bornless servant...," He nearly stumbled over the words, "...*Agathodaimon Ereschigal*, bound hereunto her seal invoke..."

This was clearly contract language, but it was archaic and scrawled in what must have been a palsied hand. Some of the words were gibberish, others were so illegible that they resembled symbols.

The girl was still upset, but the nonsense was spoiling the mood. Worse, the letter's insane ramblings might present sufficient grounds to challenge the will, regardless of the added clause.

Something slid from the envelope and clattered onto the

desk. It was an opalescent gemstone set in dull metal. Diana's breath caught in her throat. Martin realized that he had looked up at her sudden silence. She stared at the stone, without blinking, for a long interval measured by the relentless thump of a raspy antique mechanism somewhere beyond the circle of light.

He looked back at the stone and noticed that its surface was etched with the symbols from the letter. Martin didn't know much about precious stones, but this looked more like a cameo brooch than one of those famous crown jewels with their own monikers. Was this the irrevocable gift? Perhaps the old woman had meant to list the heirloom as the 'Agatha Diamond'.

With that assumption, he pushed on with the letter, "... and Ereschigal, full satisfied, leap the threshold, with shadowless eyes, whose mouth ever flameth..." Martin cleared his throat, stalling for time. He didn't recognize the term 'Ereschigal' from the context or any of the previous estate planning documents. It could be the name of a mega-yacht. Hell, it may even be an exotic private island.

Martin was experienced with assets that needed to be hidden for financial or legal reasons. If the girl wanted it, she'd have to come clean.

"Do you understand what this is regarding?"

Diana continued to stare at the peculiar gemstone. "Ereschigal is our family...servant."

"The butler? With the white hair?"

"You haven't seen this one yet. And you won't." She dragged her eyes off the desk and looked him in the face. "I want you to leave."

Martin settled back in the throne. "I haven't even finished reading the will."

"I know my grandmother's will. I have money of my own, I'll pay you to walk away."

They had arrived at the bargaining stage. Martin leaned forward. He didn't care about money, and he loved to watch that dawn on the faces of his wealth obsessed opponents. Their impotent rage was so exquisitely delicious.

"I am not leaving until you have accepted your grand-mother's terms. If you don't, I'll be forced to take the matter to probate court. The estate will be tied up for years, while relatives and creditors comes sniffing around with lawsuits of their own. The entire fortune will be bled dry just maintaining the assets. You will lose everything, I assure you."

Diana reached for the gemstone.

Martin pulled it away. "It's yours. All you have to do is," he looked down and finished reading the letter, "...consign this wretch to bane and bale."

Martin watched her thin shoulders slump. As much as he relished the fight, he savored the look of defeat.

Diana said, "Very well, Grandmother. Thy will, be done."

Martin set the paper down for her signature.

Diana reached past the pen and picked up the dagger.

INKY'S DAY OUT

Groups of costumed children skipped through the shimmering twilight, eyes peeled for man-eating monsters. Pale things hovered around them and hungry, bug-eyed creatures crept among the mossy stones. Yasmine waved to them. She knew all the slimy, spiny, scaly critters in the bubbling tanks. The aquarium was her home away from home.

"Children, no running. Kids...*Niños!*" Yasmine's teacher shouted at her unruly classmates. The aquarium was the only attraction in town, and the kids had all been there for birthday parties and weekend outings, not to mention every other field trip. They were tired of it, and besides, it was Halloween! Nobody cared about a bunch of ugly fish on the best day of the year.

A volunteer in a blue uniform and a headset microphone called out, "Who wants to see a special Halloween surprise?"

That got their attention. The kids clustered around a wide glass wall and stared into the murky water.

Yasmine, a dark-skinned girl in a homemade octopus costume, sat at the edge of the group. She knew this was the Giant Pacific Octopus tank. She knew the volunteer giving the presentation. She could have even given the presentation herself, so she tuned it all out and studied the swaying reeds, lumpy coral, and speckled sand. Somewhere in there a master of camouflage was hiding.

"...can travel great distances in search of food." The volunteer paused, seeing a boy with his hand up. "I'll be happy to answer your questions after our special presentation."

The teacher tapped the boy on his shoulder. "Save it for later, Donnie."

Donnie wasn't wearing a costume. He'd been in a bad mood since that morning when his costume had been confiscated. Of course, the only part of his costume he'd decided to bring was a giant futuristic laser gun.

He kept his hand up. "Hey, I got a question!"

The volunteer smiled. "Yes?"

"Uh, why is this so boring?"

A group of boys around him laughed. Yasmine's teacher bent down and said something stern, punctuating her words with a straight finger.

"Oh, look!" The volunteer looked over her shoulder. "Just in time for Halloween!"

A pair of hands lowered a large orange pumpkin into the tank. It bobbed for a moment and then sank, trailing silver bubbles from a few small holes.

"As I said, our octopus, Inky, is highly intelligent and very curious. This will provide stimulation and something for him to explore."

Yasmine saw it first. A rough gray lump clinging to a rock pile that blushed with a rich ruby color. The octopus launched towards the pumpkin. The kids finally noticed as Inky floated by, filtering the light through the red webbing that radiated from his large swollen head.

Inky searched the pumpkin with his curling arms, checking to see if it was some tasty new kind of clam.

Donnie hammered on the glass with his fist. "Boo!"

Inky shrank and his skin became smooth and orange, blending against the side of the pumpkin.

Yasmine jumped up before she knew what she was doing.

"Leave him alone!"

Donnie had bullied her many times and she'd never once stood up for herself, but she refused to let him frighten a poor innocent creature. Inky was only three years old! Technically that was old for an octopus, but that didn't make it right.

"Inky is smart," She said, her voice squeaky but fierce. "If you scare him he'll remember and be afraid of us." She waved her arms as she spoke, which pulled the strings attached to fake purple arms that flopped around.

Donnie sneered. His shirt that day coincidentally featured a cartoon shark bursting from a neon blue wave and screaming 'Gotta Eat 'Em All!'

"Naw'uhhh. Octopi are stupid."

Their teacher fumed. "Donnie, that's enough out of you."

The volunteer held up her hands for Yasmine's teacher to hang back. She and the other volunteers knew Yasmine well. She was confident that this was one area where the young girl was in control. The boy had stepped into the deep end of the pool, so to speak.

Yasmine put her hands on her hips, and her other arms followed. "First, the plural of octopus is octopuses, because the root word is Greek, not Latin. Second, the octopus is the smartest invertebrate on the planet. They use tools, like dolphins and chimpanzees. They even have nine brains, if you count the smaller ones that control each arm. They also have three hearts and blue blood. They're practically an advanced alien species!"

Donnie flinched, and then clenched his jaw. "Durrr, here's a fact...a shark would win a fight with an octopus every time!"

He ripped the threads from the side of her costume. Three of her purple arms dropped lifelessly to her side. Yasmine burst into tears.

The teacher separated them and gave the volunteer a withering look.

Inky watched it all from behind the pumpkin. He didn't know that there were little sharks in the dry part of the aquarium, and he'd been even more surprised to see the purple octopus out there.

The shark had looked scared before it went on the attack. It was all so strange, not to mention this big orange ball in his tank. Inky had a lot to think about.

The children left soon after with the rest of the crowds. The volunteers and staff rushed through their evening responsibilities to get home for Halloween. The lights in the aquarium dimmed. It was time for Inky to make his move.

He scrunched his body up and squeezed through a hole in the pumpkin. Once inside, he used his siphons to pump out some of the water, and then he plugged the holes with his suckers. The bubble of trapped air sent the pumpkin bobbing back to the surface of the tank.

Inky shoved the lid off, hoisted up the pumpkin and then lowered it over the side. The pumpkin was full of water. He would need it while he explored the dry side of the aquarium. If that other octopus could roam around, Inky could too.

The pumpkin rolled down a long wheelchair ramp all the way to the main entrance. A janitor wedged the door open with his supply cart.

He leaned around the corner. "Hey, am I supposed to toss this pumpkin?"

When he looked back, the pumpkin was gone. He shrugged and locked the door.

Inky rolled down the street, taking in the sights of the strange dry world. People out there lived in enormous holding tanks with only a few glass panels. None of the plants were familiar, and he didn't see any fish except for the big lamp-eyed whales that cruised over the long black paths. Luckily there were only a few of those. But there were so many people! There were a few tall people, but most of them were young and small.

Inky had seen them every day of his life. They always pressed their faces up against his tank and smeared the glass with their sticky fingers. He thought that all young people looked the same, but tonight they came in every shape, texture and color. There were green-skinned ones with pointy black heads, red ones with little spikes and white ones that flowed like jellyfish. Inky watched them approach a big person holding tank.

They touched the wall and a tall person came out and gave them something. This made the young ones happy, so it was probably fish heads or crab legs.

Inky wanted some fish heads too.

He waddled across the driveway and hefted his pumpkin up the steps. There was a little spot on the wall that shined like a pearl. Inky stretched his arm and pressed a sucker against it.

There was a short musical chime. A moment later, the door opened.

Inky panicked and withdrew into his pumpkin.

"Eh, hello?" A very handsome man, with a large smooth head and loose wrinkled skin, shuffled to the door. "Anyone there?"

The man looked around for a moment and then shut the door.

Inky reached up and pressed the music spot again.

This time the door opened faster. The handsome man looked around. "Hello? Tricks again? Hooligans!"

He slammed the door.

Inky reached up. Before he could touch the button the door jerked open.

The handsome man yelled, "A-ha!"

Inky pointed his siphon, ready to squirt ink in case the man tried to eat him.

"Yasmine, is that you?" He chuckled. "Back for seconds? Well, I don't see why not."

He reached for a bucket and poured some treats into Inky's arms.

"Have a happy Halloween...and watch out for those hooligans."

Inky tasted the food with his suckers. They weren't like any fish he'd ever had before. They were gummy like jellyfish and impossibly sweet. He wondered what they were giving away at the next place. He propped the pumpkin up with six of his arms and headed down the path.

A husky voice boomed, "Die, aliens!"

The sound was familiar and scary. Inky saw two more pumpkins along the path, so he pulled his close and curled up inside.

Donnie galloped down the street in a green plastic army

helmet with a camouflage shirt and pants. His shirt said 'Space Marine' in black magic marker. He pointed his laser rifle at the first pumpkin.

"Destroy the alien egg sacs!" He ran over and stomped on the pumpkin, kicking its yellow guts across the yard.

His two friends laughed. They were also dressed in camo. All the boys had more pumpkin on their combat boots than they had candy in their bags.

"Hey, look who it is," one of them snickered.

"Shhh, let's hide!" Donnie said.

Yasmine skipped down the sidewalk. Her father had fixed her loose arms with bendy wire. Now they curled in the air like real octopus arms, and one of them held her sack of candy. She slipped on the shattered pumpkin.

Donnie and his friends pointed and laughed.

Yasmine sat up, leaking candy from her torn bag.

"Watch out, octopus," Donnie said, "or you might get squashed!"

He dropped his heel on the second pumpkin and smashed it like an egg.

Yasmine tried to get up, but her real arms were tangled in her fake ones. "Leave me alone!"

"What, are you gonna cry to the teacher?" He looked around. "Hey guys, do you see a teacher anywhere?"

They laughed and crowded around her.

"Why don't you tell us another fact, nerd?"

Yasmine narrowed her eyes for a moment, looking at the boys and their costumes.

"Okay, Donnie. The fact is...you're secretly scared of aliens."

Donnie's friends looked up at him. His face puckered, like he'd been caught chewing on a lemon. "What? N'ah-unh!"

Inky peeked out of his pumpkin and was delighted to see that other purple octopus! He uncurled all eight of his dripping wet arms and waved 'hello!'

Donnie dropped his laser gun and ran shrieking into the

night. His friends scrambled too, so fast they left their helmets spinning on the ground.

Yasmine gasped, "Inky? What are you doing out here?"

Inky pulled her knotted strings loose and set her free.

She scooped up his pumpkin. "Come on, let's get you back where you belong."

Inky picked a gummy fish off the street and squeezed it in his suction cups.

"You want to keep trick-or-treating?"

Inky turned his body green and held black arms over his head like a pointy witch hat.

Yasmine giggled. "Well, I guess we can hit a few more houses. It is your first Halloween."

They strolled into the shimmering twilight arm in arm, in arm, in arm, in arm.

RED SNOW

Rose checked her Halloween makeup in the car mirror one last time and then zipped up her parka. Her mother scanned the frosted windows before letting her out.

"Don't stay too long. It's getting dark early."

Rose rolled her eyes. "I know, Mom. It's darker like, every day."

"And Mrs. Brower is still driving you home?"

"Yes. I'll be fine." She leaned over and pecked her mom on the cheek, leaving behind a smudge of green face paint.

"Remember, you can call me if you need anything."

Rose opened the door. "Is your number still 911?" She hopped down into the snow. "I'll try to save you some candy, bye!"

Sheriff Lena Nageak watched her daughter skip across the frozen street to the community center. A cruel wind shrieked off the Arctic Ocean and tried to snatch her floppy witch hat, but Rose held tight and made it inside.

The Sheriff started her patrol.

A few trucks and snowmobiles rumbled past, but the streets were mostly empty. The real harvest festival in their tiny Alaskan town was *nalukataq*, when the local *Iñupiat* people celebrated a successful bowhead whale hunt. It was late in the season, however, and there had not been a festival.

Some of the native whaling crews were staying out on the ice pack, desperately waiting for a catch. The bowhead whale was a much needed source of food in a place where a weeks' worth of groceries cost five hundred dollars. Everything cost more above the Arctic Circle because all of the supplies had to be flown in.

In spite of the brutal cold there was more ice melting every year, and so the whales traveled further out at sea. The town itself was slipping beneath the rising water, its young people were leaving to seek opportunity elsewhere, the elders were dying, and their culture was withering away. The town was already weak and depleted, and the long dark winter was closing in.

Her daughter was right. Things were getting darker every day.

* * *

Rose kicked the snow off her boots and hung up her parka. The community center was her warm oasis.

Most of the other kids spent the snowy months snow-mobiling, hunting and ice fishing, but her mom never let her do any of that. There was only school, church and basketball. Everything needed a chaperon and a reliable drop-off and pick-up time. She'd spent many hours here alone, doing homework while she waited up for her mother.

Rose saw some of her friends in the corner and squealed. She didn't need the sun as long as she could see them.

She skipped past the black and orange streamers. Some of the village elders were there, gossiping in *Iñupiaq* or *Yu'pik*. They laughed at Rose's costume, smothered her with hugs and offered her cubes from their bags of fried whale blubber. She let the *muktuk* melt in her mouth, but it was soured by the guilt of knowing how little was left.

* * *

Sheriff Nageak lowered her window for the lean teenage boy flagging her down. Pete Weyapuk stood astride his snow-mobile and lifted his goggles. His eyes were bleary but wide. His family and the Browers had been camped out on a large ice floe for weeks.

"Sheriff! The DCW and NOB crews need help!"

She flinched. "*Auniq*?" Rotten ice, thin and melting.

Pete nodded.

She grabbed her radio. "I'll call Search and Rescue. Get home and stay safe." She reported the news as she bounced across the pitted permafrost road out to the police station.

She spotted something along the frozen shoreline on the outskirts of town. A long streak in the snow glinted red in the last smudges of sunlight. She prayed it wasn't one of the whalers.

She grabbed her shotgun and hustled through the frost covered forest of whale bones that jutted from the ice. What few parts of the whale that could not be used were dumped here on the far edge of town. The carcasses were old, picked clean and frozen solid. There should be no trace of fresh blood.

The gory trail came from nowhere and simply ended. She circled around in a wider search pattern and then she saw them, a pair of small dark eyes. It was the head of a baby polar bear.

She straightened up and scanned the white void with her shotgun.

The whale carcasses were left here to keep any scavengers away from town. As the sea ice diminished it became harder for the polar bears to hunt seals, and so they had come to rely on these leftovers more with every year. But this year there had been no whale harvest, and there was nothing to scavenge here but dry bones. The bears must be starving now if they were forced to eat their young.

The Sheriff tried to remain clinical as she examined the scene, but she was drawn back to the baby's eyes. Trapped beneath their frozen skin was the vision of the bear's mother eating it alive. She shook it off and followed the bloody tracks. The prints were deep and wide, dwarfing her boots, each tipped with the grooves of long sharp claws. The trail headed straight towards town.

She had to coordinate the search and rescue operation, but someone had to locate that bear. She got back in her truck and notified Wildlife Management. Her foot hovered over the gas pedal. She looked back at the streak.

The arctic sea snuffed out the sun, the snow faded to blue and the bloody streak turned black. She still felt the frozen pools of the little bear's eyes on her, shining with the red reflections of its mother's maw.

She gripped the steering wheel. A clammy feeling coiled around her stomach. It was not a stabbing panic or creeping dread. It was something worse; it was certainty.

She cranked the wheel and sped back towards town.

* * *

Rose and her friends chewed licorice whips and laughed together. The music had been stopped for a raffle that dragged on in the background. One of the elders called out numbers, but no one was there to claim the prizes.

"Isn't that you?" Rose's friend grabbed her ticket. "Oh my god, you won!"

Rose looked up and remembered the raffle.

The elder called her up. Rose noticed that the community center had nearly emptied out.

"Congratulations, Rose!" The elder pointed to a duffel bag on the prize table.

Rose looked inside. "Wow!" There must have been thirty pounds of deer meat inside. "My mother loves venison. Thank you!" She hugged the elder and rejoined her friends.

They were already pulling on their jackets. Word had spread about the crews stuck on the ice, and so everyone was headed home.

Her friend asked, "Need a ride?"

"I have one...um, happy Halloween, you guys."

The remaining people drained from the community

center. Rose tried to find Mrs. Brower before realizing that she must have rushed home when she'd heard the news. The lights clicked off around her. Rose really didn't want to call her mom for a ride in the middle of a rescue operation.

She was a big girl, she could walk home by herself. She hefted the meat onto her back and headed out into the deepening twilight.

The streets were empty and quiet. Even the constant drone of snowmobiles was missing. There was no sound but the wind cutting between the wooden buildings and the hollow crunch of snow underfoot. She put her head down and hiked.

Rose rarely got this much time to herself. Her mom kept her schedule full and never let her wander out of sight. She wondered when she'd be able to get a job. Maybe she could pitch it as a way to help out with the bills and learn some independence. Yeah right, that would go over well.

She huffed and watched her breath vanish in the wind. Her mom was always busy during the holidays, so all of Rose's favorite Halloween memories involved her father. In the photos he wore a ridiculous costume and a big goofy grin. Her mom never got that silly, being a cop and all, but she definitely used to smile. There were pictures to prove it.

The smiles stopped when they lost her father.

A plastic jack-o-lantern grinned at her from the window of a darkened house.

"Happy Halloween, I guess."

The wind yanked off her witch hat and dragged it down the street. Rose turned to chase it and then stopped. There was an odd smell on the wind. She had no idea what it was, but she started walking faster.

＊ ＊ ＊

Sheriff Nageak listened to the rescue operation over the radio as she drove, eyes darting to her shotgun. It was loaded with less-than-lethal rounds for scaring off 'nuisance' bears. She leaned over to grab a box of 12 gauge slugs from the glove compartment.

The truck fishtailed on a patch of ice. She got it under control and then pulled over. She quickly swapped the ammunition. She needed to be armed and ready when she got to town.

The radio crackled. "Call off the snowmobiles and sleds. The ice is too treacherous."

She grabbed the radio. "Where are we on the boats?"

"We got a dozen scrambling from town."

She looked out at the ocean and imagined the people trapped in the dark, listening while the thin layer between them and the abyss groaned and splintered.

When her husband had gone missing, the entire community had joined in the search effort. They'd nourished her hope with constant encouragement. A plane eventually located the tracks of his snowmobile. They led to a gaping patch of rotten ice.

The community held a few prayer vigils and then set their draglines downstream. Lena had clung to the hope that they'd at least recover his body. She'd stood for hours balanced on that thin edge of ice, staring into the black water. The relentless razor wind had stripped away her hope and exposed it as foolish denial. The cold seeped inside and filled her with one merciless certainty; once a thing is gone, you never get it back.

She set the loaded shotgun on the seat beside her and pulled back onto the road.

* * *

Rose listened to the crunching footsteps that followed each of her own. There were too many. Sound never echoed out here on the tundra. She kept her head down and kept moving, too afraid to turn around.

The gauzy layers that had been drifting off the mountains

were now thick clumps of snow that flew sideways, stinging her exposed face. She ducked behind a shed to catch her breath. She hadn't gone far but she was already exhausted. Rose thought about dropping the heavy bag of deer meat. A flicker of shame warmed her belly. Throwing away food while people all around her went hungry would be unforgivable. She forced herself back onto the road.

The crunching behind her had stopped. Maybe it had just been her imagination. She risked a look around the street. It was still empty. She continued towards home.

Rose knew that the days were getting shorter but it was unsettling how the night had prowled into town, as though it could no longer wait. The darkness was close and heavy, part of the winter that would soon devour the sun.

She noticed that her feet were making no sound in the fresh snow. Maybe those footsteps behind her hadn't really stopped at all.

Something moved across the street. Rose caught a glimpse of dark fist-sized shapes that evaporated in the heavy snow. Different parts of her brain clamored for her attention. She was about to listen to the comforting voice that assured her that nothing was wrong, but then she saw it. Her entire body screamed at her to run.

She sprinted down the middle of the road, lungs gasping with searing cold air. The polar bear moaned and galloped after her, enormous but gaunt, more terrifying than any healthy animal. Its skeleton strained against its rippling mangy cloak, propelled by maniacal starvation.

Rose turned onto a side street and wiped out on the ice. She tossed the bag of deer meat and frantically crawled the other away.

The starving polar bear stopped to sniff the duffel bag.

Rose looked around for a place to hide. The houses were on short stilts to keep them from sinking into the permafrost in summer. She crawled underneath one and waited for the polar bear to leave.

The bear pawed at the bag and snorted. The meat was too lean to provide much sustenance. It raised its long neck and continued to sniff the air for Rose.

* * *

Sheriff Nageak rolled into town with one hand on the shotgun and her cell phone on her lap. She called Rose again. It continued to ring, unanswered.

A pale shape swept across the beams of her headlights. She hit the brakes and slid, gripping the shotgun. She squinted through the frosted windshield. There was nothing but a phantom of snow departing on the wind.

A block later she spotted something torn apart in the middle of the street. She lowered her window halfway and aimed her flashlight at it. It looked like a duffel bag and a few scraps of meat.

Rose's voice chirped through her phone's speaker. "Hi, this is Rose. Sorry you missed me!"

She hung up and dialed again. The faint sound of Rose's cell phone drifted on the wind. She jumped out, shotgun at the ready, and followed the familiar ringtone. Huge bear tracks dented the fresh snow.

The ringing stopped. Her daughter's voice faded to a whisper the further she went from the truck. "...Sorry you missed me..."

She walked in the bear prints and scanned beneath the houses with her flashlight. She caught the gleam of a cell phone.

Maybe it wasn't her daughter's phone. Maybe Rose had dropped it when she got away. That cold certainty tugged at her bones. She looked down. She was surrounded by red snow.

TOP TEN TIPS TO GET YOUR BODY READY

Are you ready to get lean? I mean *absolutely shredded*?

If you're dedicated to health and fitness, you've spent years maintaining your body in order to enjoy an active lifestyle. But what about the afterlife? You *can* take it with you! A rich and fulfilling afterlife is possible for those willing to put the work in ahead of time.

Here are ten tips for becoming a <u>Spooky Scary Skeleton</u>.

1) **Rock Solid:** Strong skeletons are made of strong bones. Weight bearing exercises will build up your bone density and strengthen the ligaments that hold your joints together. A skeleton's teeth are also on display, so you'll want to avoid sugar and stay on top of dental hygiene. Be sure to meet your hydration needs now, because anything you drink as a skeleton will pour right through you. Most importantly - calcium, calcium, calcium.

2) **Feel the Music:** Learn an instrument. At a minimum, every proper skeleton should be proficient with the xylophone. Once you have mastered the rudiments of percussion, every bone becomes a drumstick and every skull becomes a drum. Did you know that skeletons don't need lips or lungs to play flutes or brass instruments? Doot-Doot!

3) **Use Your Head:** If you want mad skull skills, up your game and start bowling, dust off the old hacky-sack, practice basketball tricks and free throws or learn juggling. It is important to commit these skills to muscle memory before your muscle is gone.

4) **Get It Together:** Learn anatomy! It will be crucial if you need

to reassemble your skeleton. Once you know the rules, you can break them. With 206 bones to play with you'll be able to re-arrange them in countless ways to express your own unique style.

5) **Skeleton Crew:** Spooky skeletons spend the majority of their time aboveground dancing, playing music, and pulling highly-coordinated pranks. It's hard to practice synchronized move-ments alone, so you should network with other would-be skel-etons. If you can form lifelong bonds you may even be buried side-by-side. Teamwork makes the scream work! It's never too early to learn choreography, but you may want to wait before swapping craniums.

6) **Grave Matters:** To find a thriving cemetery, consider things like weather and landscape. Nobody wants to claw their way through frozen ground or have their bony antics missed against a backdrop of snow. Look for loose soil and bent creepy trees with a healthy population of owls, crows and bats. Take note of the tombstones; are they good for hiding behind and jumping on?

7) **The Eyes Have It:** It is rare to become a skeleton with your eyes intact, which is why this feature is so striking. If you think your eyes will go the way of all flesh, getting a glass eye now could be an investment in your future.

8) **Crawl In Together Now:** Another easy way to accessorize your look is with an exotic pet like a rat, snake or spider. Make sure to specify in your will that your beloved pet should be bur-ied with you.

9) **Spine Up:** Before you die, make sure that you have registered with the Skelective Service. You may be drafted into the Skel-eton War. If you do not wish to be buried in chain mail, you should at least pack a shield and weapon in your coffin. Spears

and swords are classics because they work even when rusty.

10) **Live Fast, Die Young:** Try not to die too violently. You only have one skeleton! Sure, a single crack in the skull can be stylish, but remember how hard you've worked for this. Don't cremate, appreciate! And when they close that coffin lid, try to get some rest. You won't have a lot once you become a Spooky Scary Skeleton.

ON MOONLIT RAILS

A bloated fly threw itself against the sun glazed windows of the Hancock Bank & Trust, buzzing as it struggled to escape into the dusty air of the Texas mining town. A portly well-dressed Englishman, Harlan Smithee, tried to conduct business on a table in the corner of the lobby. He reeled a pair of buyers towards a display of gold trinkets spread across a green silk cloth.

"You could melt these beauties down or display them in your finest museum. Available now for a fraction of their value!"

One of the shoppers, a skinny old codger in a bowler hat, squinted and lifted his wire frame spectacles. "You must have twelve ingots worth there! Which mine did you get this from?"

Harlan smiled, compacting his jowls. "No mine in the U.S. territories offer riches such as these."

The other shopper, who was older than the first, gave a harrumph that stirred his white whiskers. "Looks like fool's gold to me."

Harlan cradled a piece in his hands and presented it for closer inspection. "Quite the opposite, good sir. This is royal treasure, crafted in ancient Egypt!"

The man in the bowler licked his lips. "Egyptian gold, you say? Surely you wouldn't object to visiting my shop tomorrow, for a simple chemist's test?"

Harlan's smile slipped. "Very good, sir. Tomorrow then."

* * *

Later that night, Harlan lay in a rented four poster bed, clutching a golden scepter to his chest in one hand and an empty bottle of whisky in the other.

"Bloody idiots. Panning for gold flakes when they could hold the scepter of a king! Sodding...pig...farmers."

He passed out, looking like a Pharaoh in repose.

He dreamt of a jaundiced moon, dark craters glaring from its ancient dome as it loomed over a black ocean. A plume of sea spray broke the surface to reveal the path of a leviathan. The luminiferous mass was serpentine yet surging straight ahead, relentlessly churning across the sea.

The chop of waves and sizzling water rose like a chorus. A chugging, rattling, clanking burst of steam shrieked, *"Haaaarlaaan Ssssmitheeeee."*

He snapped awake into harsh daylight and the clatter of someone knocking at his door.

"Mister Smithee? There's a telegram for you at the Post Office."

✻ ✻ ✻

Harlan stood in front of the post office, chilled with sweat despite the oppressive Texas sun. He re-read the telegram.

M. SMITHEE
YOUR COLLEAGUE REG. ELLWORTH HAS DIED STOP AS SOLE SURVIVOR OF CAIRO EXPEDITION PLEASE ADVISE ON CURATION OF EGYPT COLLECTION

A steam whistle pierced the air, signaling the shift change at the mine. Harlan looked over his shoulder and folded up the telegram.

✻ ✻ ✻

Harlan waited inside a wooden store front and watched the street from a picture window frosted with the letters "Collectibles and Consignments".

The man in the bowler hat leaned over the gold artifacts with a glass vial.

"It's solid gold, as good as your word, Mr. Smithee."

Harlan slouched into a chair with a sigh of relief. He scratched his sweaty hair and hiccupped a burning mouthful of gin.

His speech slurred, revealing his buried cockney accent. "Like I says, yours for a song. Just book me a passage on the first coach east in the morning."

The old man traced the curves of a gold ankh medallion with a jeweler's loop.

"We have a deal! Tell me more about these pieces, Smithee. Perhaps I could make more by shilling them to curiosity seekers than by melting them down."

"Ain't you 'eard about them pharaohs?"

"I read the Bible. I know my pharaohs from the Pharisees."

"But did you know, even though them royals 'ad all the wealth in the world, they didn't spend it?"

"And why not?"

"They needed it for the afterlife, right? When they died they was mummified, organs pulled out, wrapped 'ead-to-toes like sausages, all so they could enjoy their gold and finery for eternity."

The old man gave him a sly grin. "Until you found it, eh?"

"Me and my colleagues, right, we was working for the Society for Archeology. We was surveying a pyramid when we stumbled upon a maze of burial chambers."

Harlan's eyes glazed over with fond memories.

He'd had far less girth and wealth back then, but that was about to change. He and his fellow group of Brits were hungry for glory and treasure, and when they peered through that gap in the granite blocks the stagnant air of the chamber beyond scintillated with such marvels that it made them salivate. They saw rows upon rows of grand sarcophagi surrounded by golden relics. A statue of the jackal-headed god Anubis stood guard, but its teeth were dull and dusty and its forbidding eyes had cobweb cataracts.

"We took enough gold and relics to fill a whole freight train and 'alf the bloody Museum of London!"

A long line of Egyptian porters loaded the sarcophagi and crates of plunder onto a procession of freight cars.

"There was no way the Egyptian government would let us take that treasure, so we steamed straight through the night on moonlit rails. We 'ad to reach the port of Alexandria before sun up.

"We burned everything we 'ad just to keep the engine going. We even 'ad to resort to burning mummies! I must 'ave cremated a 'undred pharaohs, and they made for fine kindling, I tell you. I can still smell that sweet resinous smoke."

The old buyer laughed and clapped his hands. "What a grand tale! Secret treasures stolen from the bony hands of dead kings and a daring midnight ride! I'll charge 'em a dollar just to get in the door!"

He paid Harlan with a sack of money and ushered him out.

"Safe journey east. I hear St. Louis is lovely this time of year. Fare well."

Harlan staggered down the dirt strip at the center of town. "Just a quick stop at the saloon and then off to the livery. I'll be on the first coach in the morning."

A baleful ray of light stabbed down at him.

Harlan watched as the face of the moon breached the coal-black clouds and looked down upon him with cratered eye sockets.

He rubbed his bleary eyes and then screamed. "Merciful God!"

He dropped the sack of money and ran. It was not the moon. It was a spectral locomotive, breathing black smoke.

The drunks and outlaws along the road saw the hysterical Englishman flailing down Main Street, nothing more.

Harlan looked back. The train was closing on him, and he could see the rotten faces of Egyptian nobles leering from its windows.

He put every ounce of hope into one last burst of speed.

He tripped.

Harlan rolled over to face the charging train, hands up and eyes squeezed tight against the glaring light.

The people gathered on the sidewalks watched dumbstruck as Harlan exploded. He became a gushing wave, crashed into a red slick of mud and smeared all the way to the edge of town.

* * *

Harlan lowered his trembling hands and pried his eyelids open.

He lay on the swaying floor of a train.

The conductor loomed over him. It had a sharp black jackal head with copper eyes that blazed like solar discs. Its lips curled in a jagged bone white smile, and it gestured to a bronze-skinned pharaoh.

The pharaoh opened the firebox door to reveal the hungry flames.

THE TALE OF THE BURNING MIDNIGHT

The embers of the campfire flickered, giving little heat and just enough light to paint the children with feeble tinges of orange and red. The warm autumn winds had departed, taking the cheerful sounds of crickets with them. A thin drab line of smoke hung in the frosty air. A tall, athletic boy cradled a pine cone as if to pitch it. He let it roll from his hand with a sigh. Behind him, a girl in an expensive puffy jacket twisted her yellow hair around one manicured finger. The smallest of them, a freckled boy with unruly red hair, cleared his throat.

"I wish I had a signal out here," he said, squinting at his cell phone.

The tall boy grit his teeth. "Put that away, or I'll pound ya!"

"You know it's against the rules," the girl sighed.

"Is my older brother here? Is yours?" The boy asked. "It's just us. Can't we at least listen to music while we wait?"

She looked up. "Why the long wait, anyway?"

The big kid tossed a twig in the fire. "It always takes longer to bring a new prospect out here."

Leaves crunched behind the wall of blue-green pines. A girl in a denim jacket and brown bandana jogged into the clearing.

"I don't know guys," she huffed, "This new kid is creepy."

The red head rubbed his hands together. "Good. Aren't we bored of the same old ghost stories?"

"We love scary stories," the blonde girl said. "That's kind of, like, the whole point."

"Sure, when we were little. But you've gotta admit that

our older brothers and sisters used up all the good ones. I wanted this kid to bring in some new," he arched an eyebrow, "... *blood.*"

The girl in the denim jacket ignored him. "When we put the bag over his head he didn't react, he just put his hands behind his back. We told him we weren't going to tie his wrists and he seemed...disappointed."

The crunch of dry leaves and whisper of bending branches bled from the darkness. Everyone turned as a lanky older boy with glasses emerged. He was guiding someone into the grove, a dark slouching figure with a burlap sack over their head.

The hooded figure pulled away and went straight towards the fire. The others jumped up, expecting the new kid to stumble into the burning logs. The figure stopped to bathe in the pulsing light. The sack rippled with quickened breathing.

The other kids looked around with wide eyes. The red head pumped his fist.

The boy with the glasses said, "All of us come from different backgrounds, different schools. One thing unites us, our love of horror. If we like your story, you will become a member of the Late Night Society. Are you ready?"

The hood bobbed once.

"Very well." The older boy picked up a worn leather bag, withdrew a pinch of powder, and then tossed it into the fire pit. The flames roared to life and leapt into the sky.

The new kid's voice was shrill and erratic. "I come here to offer a story for the pleasure of the Late Night Society. It is called 'The Tale of the Burning Midnight'.

"There once was a group of children that liked to gather in the woods. They huddled around a campfire telling ghost stories; Resurrection Mary, the Black Dog, Cry Baby Bridge, tales of cursed objects, haunted houses and unfinished business.

"They grew up and grew apart, changed schools, moved away. Younger siblings took their place, and they invited new kids to share the clearing. They never saw the one standing in the trees behind them, listening to their words and laughter."

Jeff C. Carter

The blond girl retreated slightly into her puffy coat.

"You don't believe that someone could hide so close to a place like this for so long, do you?"

The girl in the denim jacket crossed her arms.

"A campfire drives the shadows from a clearing, but when you face the light it makes you blind to the darkness. You may feel the heat on your front, but you never feel the eyes on your back."

The red head leaned in, entranced.

"The one in the woods grew to understand. They did not gather to listen to childish stories. They trekked through the woods and endured the weary mornings after because they hungered for fear. They drank it in with their ears until their stomachs fluttered and their hearts pounded. They drank until the well ran dry. Their skin no longer prickled. The hairs on their necks no longer rose. The fire was dwindling.

"And so, the listener came out of the darkness and stood in the light."

The athletic boy looked pale.

"Of course the listener knew about the special powder in the old leather bag. The listener distracted them with a story... and threw it all in the fire at once."

The boy with the glasses licked his lips and pulled the leather bag closer.

"The explosion lit the sky over the entire forest. When the paramedics finally arrived, they found the smoldering grove and the children who had been baptized in flames. Their clothing had melted to their bodies. Their scalps had been burned clean. Their ears, noses, lips, and tongues had all shriveled and boiled away.

"It was a miracle they had survived. The doctors thought it was because they were young, but maybe there was something strange about that grove, or perhaps there was power in that special dust. Young and old, boy or girl, there was no telling their blistered, blackened bodies apart. They were forever bound by tragedy, but they would never again be able to conjure their stories. Their mouths were scorched and empty.

"But that yearning for fear remained. In time, they realized that they had never really cared about silly children's stories. What they truly craved were squeals and howls of terror. And so they returned to the forest in darkness. They continued to bring blindfolded children into the ancient grove, to reap the sounds of horror."

The figure in the hood fell silent, yielding the night to the hungry crackle of flames.

The others looked around, stunned.

The red head leaned forward. "Wow! That was really 'meta'."

"Meta?" The girl in the denim jacket sneered.

"It was a story about a story! Man, I wish I'd thought of a story where some crazy thing happened to all of us."

"Will...happen," the hooded figure said.

The boy in the glasses shouted, "Hey, give it back!"

The hooded figure slammed the leather bag into the fire.

FULL MOON HALLOWEEN

"I know you're disappointed, but I'm proud of how you've handled the situation," Tomm's father said. "You've really improved your attitude these past few weeks."

Tomm Howard shrugged, "Well, uh, it's like you're always saying, 'you can't control everything...'"

His father finished along with him, "only how you react.'" He patted Tomm on the shoulder. "We'll have our own Halloween party in the morning. I'll make pumpkin pancakes." He unlocked the reinforced steel door to the basement. "Self-control is even more important now that you're a werewolf." The door squealed open. "Fortunately, we all have shackles for nights like these."

"Yeah," Tomm rubbed the back of his neck. "Would it be okay if I locked myself in my own cell tonight? Seeing you and mom wolf out is, uh..."

His father shook his head. "I get it, you're too cool to watch your mother and old man burst out of their clothing. That's fine, just keep your music down. We don't want any trick-or-treaters knowing that we're home."

"Got it. Thanks, Pops. Happy Halloween." Tomm ran upstairs to his private cell.

He turned on some music, opened his closet and smiled. After weeks of working in secret, his Halloween costume was finally done. He was going out. He was going to a costume contest. And he intended to win.

The steel door to the basement clanged shut. Tomm eased his own door closed and snuck out of the house.

The honeyed light flowed around him, languid and gold.

The rustle of fiery boughs and patter of falling acorns swelled before him like applause, and the breeze beckoned him onward with warm kisses scented with burning leaves.

Tomm was oblivious to these splendors of autumn. He was dimly aware that his blood felt fizzy, like Mountain Dew, but not because of the stupid moon. It was Halloween and he was going to a party. No bowling, no pizza. A real party, with girls.

He'd never been popular, exactly, but he'd had a few close friends, he played basketball and even participated in a few clubs. The curse ended all of that. He only had to stay home during the full moon, but those holes in his social life added up fast. First he had to drop out of the big class ski trip, then summer camp and a dozen away games. At first he'd blamed it on his own health, then on ailing family members. He'd even made up a lie about his parents becoming Seventh Day Adventists. Nobody at school had questioned it. They simply let him fade from their lives.

Tomm had been scared to tell even his best friends the truth. Their regular hangouts trickled to a few last minute invitations. His friends would catch a midnight movie and Tomm would chain himself up in his room. The less they saw each other the more private jokes went over his head, and soon every story ended with 'I-guess-you-had-to-be-there'.

Life as an outcast was miserable, but worse still was the night of the full moon. Tomm's solitary existence was crushed so small that he even lost himself. He would cower beneath the dark sky and wait for the full moon to seize him. It stretched his flesh and twisted his bones like silly-putty to satisfy its sadistic whims.

That had become Tomm's life, but his depression had lifted about a month before Halloween. He'd loved making his costumes before, but now it was extra special. He would be back in charge of his life on Halloween. For that one night, he decided who or what he should be.

He couldn't believe his luck when he found out that one

of the seniors at his school was going to throw a raging Halloween party, and that anyone could get in if they had a costume. There was even supposed to be a contest. Tomm finally had something to look forward to. Life was good again.

Then it had all come crashing down.

His parents forbid him from going because there was going to be a full moon on Halloween.

Tomm had nearly exploded with rage, but in the end he'd simply been crushed beneath the absolute unfairness of it all.

Then he made up his mind.

He wasn't going to let the full moon take this away from him too.

Now his parents were locked safely away and Tomm was a free man.

He headed off to the store. He didn't want to show up at the party empty handed.

The doors slid open and he walked into a noxious cloud of pine and fake cinnamon. He did a double take that nearly gave him whiplash. The store was filled with Christmas trees. The animatronic lawn zombies had been swapped for grazing reindeer. The candy corn had been replaced with candy canes.

Tomm wandered the aisles of eggnog and gingerbread looking for chips and Halloween candy. The speakers overhead began to croon 'Last Christmas' by Wham!

"Oh, come on!" This was bullshit. Halloween wasn't even over and Santa was already dancing on its grave!

He slammed his fist on a shelf.

A little toy Santa activated and began gyrating to its own tinny recording of 'Santa Baby'. Tomm had the urge to spike it onto the linoleum floor but he resisted long enough to escape the store.

The sun had gone and left behind a purple canvas. It was only a matter of time until the moon showed her gloating face. He clenched his jaw and felt the grind of fangs.

He took a deep breath. His parents were freaked out over

nothing. Tomm had no reason to get upset. This was his night. He was going to a party, and his costume was awesome.

Packs of children rang doorbells up and down the street. It looked like a good way to get back into the proper holiday spirit.

He had nowhere to change into his costume, so he walked up to the first door in his jeans and flannel shirt with his bag slung over his shoulder. The house smelled vaguely of fish. The old bald homeowner squinted at Tomm with suspicion.

Tomm stepped into the light. "Um, trick-or-treat?"

The old man's face puckered with a toothless frown. "Eh? This candy is for kids. If you want some get a job, you hooligan!" He slammed the door in Tomm's face.

Tomm sighed and fell in behind a group of parents headed down the sidewalk with their kids. He stood to the side and let the kids ring the doorbell. A little round woman handed everyone a crinkly treat. He tore it open.

It was a taped up wad of pennies.

"Thanks?"

The prim couple at the next house handed him a bag of unsalted pretzels and a tiny black-and-white comic strip about Halloween called 'The Devil's Holiday'. Tomm spat out the first stale pretzel and dumped it all in a trash can. Why were people determined to suck the fun out of Halloween?

He took a deep breath and tried to relax. It didn't matter if the people at those houses sucked, they were just stops along the way to the party. Tomm wasn't going to let a few random jerks ruin his night.

A car screeched by and something pegged him in the back of the head.

"What the-?" His hand came away thick with clammy yellow slime. Broken egg shells crunched under his feet.

His eyes flared red as he tracked the car turning down the block. They thought they could outrun him.

Tomm sprinted through the dark woods, skipping across muddy puddles and bounding over logs. He saw every falling leaf and fluttering moth. He heard the squeals of mice scurrying beneath the underbrush. There was no escaping him now.

What kind of scum would egg someone on Halloween? What if he'd been wearing his costume?! His chest rattled with a deep growl that shook hot drool from his gnashing teeth.

He leaped over a backyard fence. The car was heading his way, unaware of what they'd unleashed. Tomm dropped his bag and flexed his hands, savoring the exquisite pain as claws erupted from his fingertips.

Moonlight shimmered off the car's windshield.

Tomm curled his jagged fingers into fists. He was not going to let the full moon destroy his night. "Don't change, don't change, stay calm, stay calm..."

The car rolled to a stop. A teenager with a feeble mustache poked his head out the window. "I swear, man. I saw something!"

A pumpkin hurtled through the darkness and shattered against the side of the car. The teenagers shrieked as the car filled with cold stringy guts.

Tomm grinned and loped away into the dark.

He heard the bongos of 'Dead Man's Party' and saw upperclassmen in costumes milling about on the porch. Tomm checked the competition. He didn't see any. He hurried in with his bag and ducked into the first bathroom he could find.

He strutted out twenty minutes later, eyes and ears dilated to receive praise and attention. High-fives might be tricky with his elaborate costume. He was dressed as two people, specifically Luke Skywalker carrying Yoda on his back. Tomm wore Luke's beige sweat-ringed tank top and khaki pants, with a fake head and mop of blond hair attached to his chest. His own head was painted green with a bald cap and pointy ears, and it projected from the Muppet body attached to his back.

A guy in a Clark Kent outfit looked him up and down. "Dude, what are you supposed to be?" He snapped his fingers. "Ohhh, I get it. Cool zombie, bro."

Tomm winced as the Halloween songs changed to pop

music and the volume shot up ten-thousand percent. Couldn't they play this normie stuff every other night of the year? He supposed it didn't matter once everyone's eardrums leaked from their skulls like grape jelly. He hoped that the costume contest would be soon.

A gang of tall guys clustered in the kitchen drinking plastic cups of beer. A dark-haired upperclassman in a tight tee-shirt smirked at Tomm. "Nice costume." None of them were dressed up for Halloween, unless the group theme was 'douche bags'. Tomm didn't think they were that self-aware.

What kind of mouth-breather went to a Halloween party to make fun of people wearing costumes? His growl was lost in the rumble of music. He waded into the crowd and relaxed. He'd never been surrounded by so many warm bodies. It must have been unclear to the party goers exactly where Tomm's body was, because people were pressing and rubbing against him. His blood was fizzing again, and he knew that all the secrecy, hard work and struggle he'd endured to get there had been worth it.

A girl slammed into him and spilled her entire cup of ice cold bud light down the front of his costume.

She looked at the fake Luke Skywalker head. "Oh my god, I'm so sorry!"

Tomm leaned over and smiled. "It's okay!"

When she saw Yoda's head move she yelped and her cup flew up, spilling the remaining beer on his pants.

Tomm laughed. She stared in wonder. "That's like, sooooo coooool..."

"Thanks. I made it myself."

She patted down his wet chest. "Oh nooooo...I totally ruined it."

"It's all good! This just looks like swamp water."

She kept her hand against his chest. It was warm and her finger nails were bubble gum pink. Her lipstick, eyeshadow and earrings were all pink, and she had a pink streak in her hair. Her pink mini-skirt was very tight.

"I loooooove Star Wars," she said.

Tomm coughed. "You do?"

"Are you like a giant baby Yoda?"

"Uh, yes. Yes I am."

"Do you know what I am?"

She did a wobbly turn to show off her costume and giggled. "Guess!"

Tomm's heart inched up his throat. Lady Gaga? Princess Bubblegum? Sexy Frankenberry?

"Can I have a hint?"

Her pink lips bowed downward. "Guess."

A shirtless guy in a plastic Spartan warrior helmet turned around. "You're 'My Little Pony', right?"

She squealed, "Yes!" and tossed her empty cup aside so that she could steady herself on the soldier's six pack abs.

Tomm narrowed his eyes as the two started to grind. He couldn't believe how rude this 'bro' was barging into their conversation. His ears prickled as they stretched into points inside the glued-on Yoda ears. Long brown hair sprouted from the skin of his arms.

He counted to ten and took slow deep breaths. If he lost his cool now a ruined costume would be the least of his worries.

"Hey everybody!" A voice clamored over the sound system. "Costume contest in the living room, come on down!"

Tomm followed people further into the house, checking his reflection along the way to make sure that both his makeup and his face were still intact.

A teenage boy in a Hawaiian shirt and pineapple sunglasses stood on top of a table with a microphone. "I'm going to call up our three finalists and then we'll vote by applause."

Tomm's fists and stomach clenched. Finalists? Had he missed something?

"All the ladies told me I have to include this guy. Spartan warrior, get on over here."

The shirtless guy strutted up to the table and flexed for the crowd. Everyone cheered but Tomm. He didn't see how a plastic helmet, red swim trunks and a pair of Birkenstock sandals could be worthy of an award. It was immediately clear to him that this whole contest was bullshit.

"Everyone loves our next competitor. It's baby Yoda!"

Tomm looked around for a second before realizing that everyone was staring at him. He awkwardly approached the host. There sure were a lot of people at this party. But he was one of the finalists! He had this thing in the bag!

"And it wouldn't be a party without our final-est finalist, Doctorrrrrrr Strange!"

The crowd parted for a figure in a flowing crimson cloak. He looked as though he'd just walked off the set of the Marvel movie. He had layers of rich blue woven robes, thick leather belts and an intricate brass medallion. His costume was flawless except for his diamond stud earrings and shiny gold watch.

Tomm scoffed. This rich kid had obviously put no effort into his costume beyond looking for the most expensive thing in the store. At least the Spartan had done sit-ups. Tomm had made and worn two costumes. He was clearly the winner.

"Make some noise if you think the Spartan is the best," the host shouted.

The ladies made a lot of noise, cat-calling as the Spartan posed his muscular, half-naked body.

"Do, or do not, make some noise for baby Yoda!"

The screaming women fell silent but a respectable round of applause took up the slack. Tomm pumped his knees in a little circle, pretending to hike through the boggy swamps of Dagobah. He got the idea to reach out dramatically, as if raising the sunken X-Wing, but the host moved on.

"What about the doctor of magic? Let me hear it!"

The roar of the crowd made the previous attempts seem like warm ups.

"Doctor Strange is the winner!"

The guy in the Doctor Strange costume nodded. The host offered him a plastic gold trophy, but he was too distracted with his cell phone to notice.

Tomm barked, "Hey!"

The crowd stopped and turned their attention back to the circle of finalists.

"He can't be the winner!" he growled.

The guy in the Doctor Strange outfit snickered. "I have the best costume, so I won. Deal with it."

Tomm's teeth crested over his snarling lips. "It's not fair! He just bought it!" Clusters of thick hair pushed through his green face paint. His rubber ears popped off and his green bald cap peeled off his bushy mane of hair.

The party goers gasped and a few yelped in surprise.

Tomm's back hunched with coiling muscles. Thick nails split through his fingers like stone arrowheads. His blood was past boiling; it had evaporated into steam and he was going to explode. This was not the pull of the distant full moon. This was molten rage at everything that was unfair in his life, including the smug prick in the fancy costume. "That's not how you... win...a costume...contest!"

He pounced and dug his claws into the rich kid, ripping and tearing until his hands were covered in a shredded red mess. He threw his furry head back and howled.

The rich kid staggered against the table, clinging to the tatters of his costume. He was nearly naked now, and it was clear that he couldn't have pulled off a costume that required abs.

The host slowly tilted the microphone back to his mouth. "I think we have a new winner, this...I don't know...two-headed Chewbacca?"

Tomm grabbed the trophy and did his best impression of a Wookie roar. The speakers resumed their deafening sonic assault and the people went back to their drinks and dancing.

The rich kid wept quietly over the ruins of his costume. "It was a rental."

Tomm strolled back into the densely packed throng holding his trophy aloft.

"Oh my god," the girl in pink stumbled towards him with

a full cup of cold beer in each hand. "I love Star Wars!"

She tripped and fell into a houseplant. Tomm slipped out of the room.

People gave him high fives and stopped to take selfies with him. He found a bucket of fun-sized candy bars and struck up a conversation with two guys in homemade ghostbuster uniforms. All of his favorite candy was already gone, these guys weren't his childhood friends, the music was still garbage and maybe he'd only won the costume contest because he had turned into a werewolf, but that was okay.

He was determined to enjoy the night while it lasted.

THE LOW DARK PLACE

The souls of the wicked drift like ash to the low dark place, where they wallow in the echoes of their sins. Harpies streak through poisoned skies over packs of ghasts as they scurry and scrap for rotten bones. Grindylows stalk the fetid swamps, where specters writhe in whirlpools of regret, and the shadmocks pierce the wind with their lonely whistle.

The new arrivals usually coalesced inside a stygian vault, but now they were bursting in as a flood of dark souls that swelled the ranks of the damned. The newcomers lined up to prostrate themselves before the titanic throne of the low dark place's first and most dreadful inhabitant, The Old One. They brought with them news of the shining world.

A horde of zombies spoke as one, commingling their dusty creaks and wet gushes into lurching speech.

"We crept to their towns...to bite the slow...ate their guts...bite the old...bite the sick. Made them like us. We spread, grew, took all their towns. They fought back. Bash skulls. Shoot guns. We got past. Found ways in. Ate the young. We took all... but the quick."

The corpses twitched, dragging thoughts from their desiccated brains.

"They learned...to cull the weak. Those left were quick... and strong. Did what they must to...wipe us out."

A chorus of howls drowned out the moans of the vanquished dead. A wave of werewolves loped forward and circled The Old One's throne. They gnashed their teeth and snarled at each other for the right to tell their tale.

The Old One turned several eyes upon the pack, singling

out the gray packmasters with their maws of worn teeth. The Old One burbled a single command.

"*Speak.*"

They passed fearful yellow glances and reached quick agreement.

"After the humans had defeated the shambling carrion, they believed that they were safe. They thought that they were survivors, but they were lambs to the slaughter! We hid among them and tainted their blood supply. When the full moon rose, ten thousand beasts awoke! Together we overran their strongholds. We ran through their bullets like spring rain. We tore through their body armor! We ripped out their spines and sucked out their marrow!"

The werewolves howled with the memory of blood on their lolling tongues.

"After the rampage, a new fear took root in the humans. Anyone of them might be one of us. They panicked and turned on each other, murdering outsiders and lynching their own. We were ready to finish them off at the next full moon."

A whimper shuddered through the army of beasts.

"But the humans found a way to test their blood. They rooted out the wolves among them. They met us beneath the next full moon with a hail of silver. In the morning, they tossed our bloody hides onto their bonfires by the thousands. When the next moon rose, there were no more wolves to sing. The humans had exterminated us all!"

They yipped and tucked their tails, pawing at the grime before The Old One's throne. Those at the back of the multitude, who had arrived last, pushed forward in silence. The flowing congregation parted like a sea of ink and bowed their alabaster faces.

A regal vampire glided up the aisle and approached The Old One's throne.

"Before you stands The Lord of Night, Lament of Mothers, merciless devourer of maidens, drinker of blood and tears... Eramus the Vicious, Emperor of Vampires!"

He gave a slight bow to the membranous entity upon the throne, and then flashed a sharp smile at his legions.

The vampires hissed in adulation.

"The surviving humans had become rather high-strung. They barricaded their homes and put their population under total surveillance. They were now battle hardened, heavily armed, and living on a hair-trigger. At last, we chose to reveal ourselves.

"We flew over their land mines and danced through their silver bullets. We invaded their safe-houses and gorged ourselves through the long red night.

"In the morning, those who had been bitten were destroyed without pity. Any enclaves that suffered heavy losses were fire bombed to purge the infected and healthy alike.

"The humans continued to adapt and evolve. They embedded their flesh with ultraviolet lights and connected themselves to machines to ensure that they were never caught sleeping. They poisoned their blood with strange chemicals to starve us, and altered their brains to remove fear and pain, along with any twinge of conscience that might make them hesitate to destroy all that was different or unknown.

"They scoured the surface of the earth and drilled into every barrow. Crypts were desecrated, catacombs were filled with fire. When I, the last great vampire, was dragged into the sun, I went laughing!"

He turned his back on The Old One, and thrust his hands out before the hideous masses. "My grand design has succeeded where all monsters before have failed. Humanity, as mankind once knew and treasured it, is no more!"

Eramus spun and pointed a taloned finger at The Old One.

"This throne belongs to me!"

The teeming rabble erupted with a roar that spread bloodlust to the far bleak edges of the realm. The vampires swarmed up the throne, followed by pouncing werewolves and the clattering dead. An endless stream of nightmares, forged and forgotten across eons, poured into the vault to vent their fury and despair.

When it was all over, The Old One's flesh lay strewn across the chamber in a quivering carpet. Eramus strode across it to take his place upon the throne.

He leaned on one elbow and spread his pale hand out for silence. The inhabitants of the low dark place bowed their gasping heads and listened.

"The twisted remnants of mankind won't last long in such a fevered state. Soon they will destroy themselves, and then…they will join us here. When they do, they will no longer be safe inside their cocoons of metal, or drunk on tonics to blunt their pain. They will arrive naked and soft as mewling newborns."

He gave them a wide, face-tearing smile.

"Let us prepare them a welcome!"

The monsters screeched and spat and wailed in anticipation of their cruel delights. When the cacophony faded, the voice of The Old One simmered from the gore puddled floor.

"You have set mankind on the path. They will travel to the stars…and explore the long forbidden places…"

Eramus looked around, unsure exactly where to fix his ire.

"…when the humans make contact with…my kind…they shall become more dreadful than you can imagine. In time, they will indeed journey to this place…and they shall not be the ones mewling."

NEARBY INCIDENTS

Karen swam through the river of news, complaints, questions and gossip that surged endlessly through her computer screen. She kept a tab open for Nextdoor, Patch, and her neighborhood's private Facebook group. Her phone buzzed with constant alerts from her Ring doorbell app, the Citizen app, as well as the local 311 Twitter accounts. Karen was not just a faceless lurker. She posted photos of suspicious people, reported graffiti, tracked nuisance dogs, and made sure that the LAPD knew damn well every time a vagrant set up camp at the bus stop.

With the exception of an amusing spat between two neighbors over an inappropriately named Wi-Fi network, it had been a slow day. The one bright spot was the news that a moving van had been spotted in front of Maureen's old place. Maureen had lived just a few doors down across the street, and Karen was delighted that someone had finally bought the place. That yard had been unkempt for years, and it had remained an overgrown eyesore after Maureen's kids had dumped her in a nursing home. Maybe now it would be managed properly.

She crossed her fingers for a quiet empty-nester, a neighbor who would keep an orderly house and not take up too much street parking. As long as it wasn't another senile hoarder, or worse, a young couple. Karen couldn't handle a parade of gender reveals, baby showers and bouncy castle birthday parties. She scrolled through her security camera footage for a sneak preview of the new arrival, but she saw nothing.

Karen clicked over to the local news station's blog. There was the usual gang violence, and a hit-and-run, but nothing in her area. She hit the Family Watchdog site to check for any new registered sex offenders. Nothing lit up her feeds like a pedophile.

No luck. She shut down everything but her security camera software and retired to the TV room. At least she had a new episode of Forensic Files.

The next day her feeds were humming with a scandal over a stolen package. Door cams had caught the alleged thief and tracked her back to a nearby house. The alleged thief was posting on-line, defending herself with a story about how her package had simply been delivered to the wrong address.

Karen's phone buzzed with news of a missing person. She ignored it and dove into her security footage to see if she had captured the thief as well.

Last night's video was fairly typical. A disgusting possum dragged its fleshy tail as it waddled down the sidewalk. She clicked over to her Facebook group to remind everyone to secure the lids of their trashcans. A black shape in the video crossed the corner of her eye. A pale stranger moved with purpose along her block. She double checked the profile of the woman proclaiming her innocence. It wasn't her. It could have been a man, one with fine features and a light step.

She noted the time. It was dark, though not particularly late. Cars were still returning from work and filing into driveways. Karen yawned and put on another cup of coffee.

By the time her Keurig had spat out the contents of a coffee pod, Karen no longer needed it. The 'Back Alley Bomber' had struck again! She had made it her life's mission to nail that son of a bitch.

The Back Alley Bomber was a notorious figure that had been defecating on her block for some time. Karen had photographed each revolting instance and cross-referenced it with security footage of the different vagabonds in the area. She had helpfully provided all of this to the police, and while there had not yet been an arrest, she had managed to get a crew from the Bureau of Sanitation out to disinfect the alleyway two blocks south.

This time her nemesis had made it personal. He had left his feces in the alley across from her home! It was almost as if he knew that it was beyond the range of her security cameras. It was the perfect crime, but not for long. Karen smiled as she ordered herself an upgraded camera set up from Amazon.

The next day she made sure her new cameras had a clear view of the alley way. Combined with her older cameras, she now had eyes on the whole block. It was time for those filthy vagrants to head for the hills. There was a new sheriff in town.

Karen neglected the police blotter and its report of another disappearance. It had happened all the way over in downtown, and besides, she knew better than anyone that when people wanted to abuse drugs and live on the street, nobody could stop them. She focused on her block and reveled in the sweeping scope of her new security system, vetting complaints about noisy leaf blowers and over-sized items discarded on the curb.

That night she skipped Forensic Files to watch the feed from her cameras. She saw the pale stranger again, and rewound him back to Maureen's old place. It was the new neighbor! She fast forwarded to see where he was headed. Her heart fluttered as he approached the alley. Could he be the Back Alley Bomber? Impossible, he had only moved in a few weeks ago.

He walked around the corner and out of sight. It was odd to see people walking in L.A. unless they were with a dog or pushing a stroller. The only other person using the sidewalk was the mailman. The neighbor must have been headed to the bus stop down that way.

In the morning she scrolled through the pre-dawn footage for any sign of the bomber. Nothing in the back alley, but on her other camera she found a hazy image of the new neighbor going into his house. She rubbed her eyes. He either worked the late shift or he was quite the night owl.

Her phone buzzed in rapid succession. All of her apps were jumping with gossip about a bizarre crime scene unfolding downtown. A homeless person had found a human head in a dumpster. All the news helicopters were hovering overhead, and someone on the Citizen app had held their phone across the line of yellow police tape to get a shot of them bagging up the head. The story trended on social media all afternoon, culminating in a prankster making the Twitter account @Mystery_ Head_LA.

Karen followed the threads and hashtags, but they were quickly buried by other shootings, armed assaults and domestic disputes. She rechecked the value of the nearby houses on Zillow. Maureen's kids had netted a pretty penny.

She copied the address and pasted it into a public records search to see what she could dig up on the new guy. She found his name on the new property record. Alexei Braun. There were no arrests, lawsuits, bankruptcies, divorces or anything else juicy like that. Mr. Braun had a very clean slate, probably because he had only recently emigrated from Rovno, Ukraine.

The only immigrants Karen knew of were the Uber drivers. She opened the app. She never used the service herself, but she liked to keep tabs on the drivers loitering in her area. She suspected that some of them supplemented their income by casing houses and robbing them later.

Mr. Braun didn't appear to own a car, so he wasn't an Uber driver. Maybe he drove a taxi?

A message popped up. The hash tags were percolating with fresh news about the mysterious head. The police had identified it as belonging to one of the people who had gone missing. Karen wondered if the others were still waiting for their heads to be found. Was there a serial killer on the loose?

She jumped over to the LAPD Compstat page and checked the crime map. Overall homicides seemed to be down, but that would change if more heads turned up. There hadn't been an active serial killer investigation in her city in years! Karen wondered what they'd call him. The Guillotine Killer? The Executioner?

She poured herself a glass of chardonnay and joined in on the gossip. The basic profile was already out there: white male, loner, travels widely...she clicked back to Mr. Braun's empty public record.

When had she seen him leave and return? She checked her videos and compared his movements with the dates of the disappearances. They lined up perfectly.

What if Braun was the killer? What if Karen was the one who solved the case? Karen wriggled in her seat and poured herself another glass of wine. She imagined herself as the star witness. She would appear as the serial killer expert on all of her favorite True Crime shows and podcasts. It felt like a dream.

It would be nothing more than that unless she gathered more evidence. She scoured her video files for Mr. Braun and logged time stamps for everything. She noticed that not only did he not have a car, which was weird enough in L.A., but he didn't seem to have a cell phone either. If he depended on Uber or Lyft, he'd have his phone out. He could have gotten around on the bus, but he always returned around dawn which was long after the local bus had stopped running.

Karen magnified her pictures of Mr. Braun. His gray suit was murky in the soft hours before sunrise. Could she find bloodstains? Signs of a struggle? She scrolled back and forth, looking for a better image. Where had he come from? She had a clear shot of him setting out in the evening, but she didn't see which way he had returned.

This could tank her whole investigation. She spent the next few hours troubleshooting her cameras. She cleaned the lenses, checked the cables, cycled the power, updated the firmware, and set everything to record in the highest possible resolution. Tonight she'd be able to see her neighbor's beady little eyes.

Her phone buzzed. An observant TV viewer had spotted something strange while searching the aerial footage from Channel Five's 'Eye in the Sky' news chopper. There was a suspicious bundle in the opening of an old industrial smoke stack not far from where the mystery head had been found. Karen pounded her fist on the table. This was supposed to be her case!

She was going to be the one to bring the killer to justice.

The police recovered several bodies from the derelict chimney. All of them had been decapitated, but they were able to match one to the head from the dumpster. The news was dubbing this the case of 'The Smokestack Killer'.

Mr. Braun left his house right on time. Karen hadn't spotted the pattern at first, because none of his movements were exactly the same, but then she realized that they were changing in lockstep with the daily drift of sunset and sunrise. Karen had developed a solid profile on this creep, and she knew when he'd return, right down to the minute. She could even go out and investigate his house while he was away, but she didn't dare. If he had half the cameras that Karen did, he would see her face, where she lived, and figure out that she lived alone.

Her own cameras were working overtime and her whining hard drive was hot to the touch. She had to stop recording and dump the bloated files a dozen times. It didn't matter, as long as she had it up and running at 5:42 a.m.

She rubbed her dry, bloodshot eyes. She felt a bit like the hard drive herself. It would be about nine hours until her neighbor returned. Karen set an alarm, put her head down on her table, and crashed.

Her phone buzzed.

It was her alarm. Karen fumbled to silence it. She had forgotten to turn on the lights. She wiped the drool from her cheek and jiggled her mouse. Her computer woke up and filled the room with cold light. She turned on her cameras and waited.

The camera's night vision rendered her street in black and white. Everything was quiet and still except for the occasional moth that streaked through the air like a distant meteor.

A shadow shifted behind a tree. Karen held her breath and zoomed in as far as she could.

Two eyes blazed from a death white face.

The possum was back.

Karen cursed and readjusted her cameras. She dimmed the glare of her monitor and checked the time. It was 5:45 a.m. She had missed Braun!

She scrolled back through the timeline for any sign of him. There was only the empty sidewalk, moths flying in reverse, and the awkward sight of the possum scuttling backwards.

She stood and plodded over to the window. The glass was cold against the tip of her nose. Karen sighed and fogged it with her breath. She raised her sweater sleeve to wipe the glass and froze.

A shaggy gray thing tumbled from the sky over Mr. Braun's driveway. It arced down hard, shuddering like a crashing kite. At the moment of impact it splayed out a pair of taloned feet.

It was impossible to tell how large the thing was. It had a hunched back and drooping bony arms. Its gray fur rippled and its spinal cord slithered against a contracting ribcage. The tapestry of animal flesh collapsed into the silhouette of a man.

Karen jabbed at her glowing monitor's tiny off button. Her flailing hand knocked over an empty wine glass.

It rang like a bell and echoed down the street.

The figure in the driveway jerked its head towards her window. It was Braun. His mouth hung open like a panting beast, revealing thick fangs and gleaming blood red eyes. His dark nostrils flared.

The possum waddled across the street in panic.

Braun tracked it with his burning eyes for a moment and then slipped into his house.

Karen clamped her shaking hand over her mouth and slid to the floor. She stayed there until her hand was slick from blubbering and the front of her sweater and her pants were both soaking wet. She did not budge until late morning had filled her home with sunlight.

Braun was a vampire. Nothing in her True Crime shows had prepared her for a monster like that.

She checked the locks on all her doors and windows, and then pushed the couch against her front door for good measure. Her hands were still shaking too much to type on her phone, but she was eventually able to order what she needed on her computer. Her first shipment of crucifixes would arrive the following day. There was a two day wait on bottles of holy water, but her grocery store could deliver garlic to her home within the hour.

Karen polished off the last of her chardonnay. She had to steady herself to face the video of last night. She watched it unwind in black and white. There was the possum, and then there was nothing. A moment later, Braun appeared as he walked up the driveway and entered his house.

There was no trace of the nightmare descending from the darkness.

Karen searched her files in vain. Her attempt to catch a serial killer had almost captured proof of a legendary monster. For some reason, she wasn't disappointed. She was in shock, of course, too numb to feel anything unless…she secretly felt relieved.

She had no evidence for the police. Karen knew from her True Crime shows that anonymous tips and uncorroborated eyewitness reports were useless.

She clicked over to the city crime stats. Homicides were still down. None of the missing people had been from her area. Karen figured that Braun was too careful to draw attention to his home.

Her phone buzzed. A case of road rage had turned into an extended police chase. It was all over social media. Other news items piled up in the sidebar. Another gang shooting. A gas station robbed by a man with a machete. A couple arrested for selling their baby. Nobody expected Karen to solve gang violence or eliminate drug abuse. All she could do was take care of herself. She continued to scroll through the news, soothed by the never ending churn of faceless tragedies.

ANONYMOUS IRL

The Facebook page 'In Loving Memory of Emma Toll' got a huge bump when the police found the rest of her body. The incoming flood of comments revealed when and where the latest details of the 'Smokestack Killings' were trending around the world. It was exactly the type of emotionally charged spectacle that David and Tyler couldn't resist.

David logged in with a fake account and typed his first comment.

bitch got what she deserved

Tyler, never to be outdone, photoshopped Emma's grinning head, taken from her high school graduation photo, onto an image of a smokestack.

The outrage was instant and intense. Within minutes, their coordinated attack had transformed the comments section from a solemn space into a raging battlefield. The conflict pulled in people from across the social network and lured an army of internet trolls from their spider holes. For every account banned, two more rose to continue the insurgency.

David and Tyler didn't really care about Emma or the Smokestack Killings. They were just in it for the 'lulz'.

David messaged Tyler in a private chat:

Look what I found.

He shared a picture of a girl at a recent soccer riot with a strong resemblance to the late Emma Toll.

Tyler responded with a yellow emoticon of a face crying with laughter.

David sipped from his liter of Mountain Dew: Code Red and smiled. Any time he could impress Tyler it was a win. In many ways they were total opposites. Yes, they were both in their twenties and spent most of their lives on-line playing video games or trolling normies. But Tyler was big, loud and confident. He didn't take shit from anyone. He'd flame them, steal their private information, and then use it to destroy them. In comparison, David was a just a pasty chinless worm. Even though he wore black tee-shirts, listened to death metal and surrounded himself with props and posters from hardcore horror movies, the truth was that he was too nervous to even look someone in the eyes.

Tyler was teaching him how to be more aggro, and how to boost his reputation within the troll community. The picture of the Emma lookalike was exactly what he needed.

He used one of his backup accounts to post the picture with the comment;

Look familiar? Emma was a crisis actor! WAKE UP America!

This bizarre claim, that the victim was actually a professional pretender, metastasized throughout the comments. Soon conspiracy theorists were debating whether the Smokestack Killings were fake news or a 'false flag' operation run by the Deep State.

Tyler took screen shots of the chaos and shared them in their favorite misanthropic forums. The anonymous members cheered David's work and passed it around the internet.

Tyler typed in the chat: U free later?

David was always free, although he rarely left his house.

yeah wussup

New drone who dis?

Sick u got it?

Yeah Mavic 2 Pro. ill bring it over after work

Not only was Tyler the only person likely to ever visit David's place, he was one of the few people who would understand it. Beneath all the horror posters were towers of gutted computers, spare hard drives, homebuilt water-cooled servers, nests of tangled cables, video game steering wheels and airplane throttle controls, old pizza boxes and a body pillow decorated with a blue haired Japanese school girl.

He showed up with a box of takeout hot wings and a heavy duty equipment case. David cracked open a fresh liter of Mountain Dew for him.

"Behold." Tyler unclipped the case's latches and raised the lid.

David pulled the hot wing from his mouth. "Whoah! That thing is sweet, dude."

Tyler lifted the sleek quadcopter from its foam cradle and prepared it for flight. "It's charged up and ready to go." He attached an impressive camera module. "Does that cute chick still live next door with her grandma?"

David took the hot wing back out. "Um, I think she moved when her grandmother got put in a nursing home. Someone else bought the place, though."

Tyler turned on the complicated remote control. "Let's meet your new neighbors."

David streamed the video feed from the drone directly to his big laptop screen. Tyler flew the drone out through the open window.

There was a gratifying rush of vertigo as the drone's camera shot straight up over the neighborhood. The treetops dwindled into clumps of broccoli and the houses shrank into monopoly pieces. Dozens of backyard swimming pools popped up like baby blue tiles among the mosaic. The setting sun dominated one side of the screen, smothering the horizon with fiery orange smog. From this height they could see which parts of the city were still basking in the afternoon glow and which were well into twilight. Tiny cars coursed along the dimming grid of streets, flicking on yellow pin prick headlights.

David laughed. "Holy shit! How high did you go?"

"We're hovering at four hundred feet," Tyler said. "If you think that's cool, check out the new camera."

He zoomed all the way in to the neighbor's squat brick house. David instinctively gripped the arms of his gamer chair as the earth rushed up into view.

Tyler grinned, "4k, bitch!"

"Huh," David leaned in towards the screen and studied his neighbor's windows, "That's different." They used to be framed with faded mustard yellow curtains. Now they were entirely black.

"I guess they wanted some privacy," Tyler smirked.

David took the hint and jumped on-line to sniff out the neighbor's Wi-Fi network and IP address. Hopping onto someone else's connection was standard practice for trolls and hackers looking to cover their trail before doing anything risky. New routers used a set number of default passwords, and some people were too lazy or stupid to install even the most basic security features. It was also a handy way to spy on someone's personal business.

"Weird. They don't have Wi-Fi. No cable, no phone, nothing." This was the digital equivalent of painting your windows black.

Tyler programmed the drone to fly in a loop high above the house. "Let me try." He reached for the laptop to employ his superior skills. "Background check has a name on the mortgage. Alexei Braun. Says he moved here from the Ukraine. Sounds like Russian mob to me."

David polished off more chicken wings. "I haven't ever seen him. Maybe he hasn't moved in yet?"

"Then who blacked out all the windows?"

"There he is!" David jabbed a sauce covered finger at his monitor. A small figure was locking the front door.

Tyler zoomed in. The door looked new, a solid slab of

modern material embedded in the old-fashioned frame. It appeared to have many locks. Alexei Braun finished and headed down the sidewalk.

"Typical euro-trash douchebag," Tyler said. He was right, Alexei had a very old world look to him. He wore a spiffy dark suit that matched his slicked back hair, and even from above, it was clear that he had thick peaked eyebrows and a pointy chin.

"No way that dude doesn't have internet," Tyler said, "unless that place is a safe house. Or a grow op."

David dabbed a sauce stain from his shirt. "You think he's growing weed?"

"Didn't you say that old lady's basement was like, insane?"

David had spent way too much time in that house over the years. When his neighbor Maureen had found out that he was 'good with computers', she'd asked him to fix every appliance she owned. It was a drag, but his mom had insisted, so he was there what seemed like once a week, resetting the clocks on her VCR and microwave, or putting her kid's numbers into her weird senior citizen cell phone. Her basement was somehow bigger than her house. It was like an old bomb shelter or root cellar, and he hated going down there to run coaxial cable or check her ancient fuse box.

"I guess you could farm weed down there," he agreed.

"One way to find out." Tyler grabbed the remote and changed the camera settings, "All the lamps would make it glow like a supernova on thermal imaging. Bam!"

The view from the drone switched to a psychedelic painting of reds, oranges and blues. The neighbor's house became a black rectangle, an open mineshaft in the vivid landscape. Tyler checked his remote. "That house is cold, as in, fucking freezing."

"What's that?" David squinted at a small blue-black blob moving down the sidewalk.

Tyler switched the camera back. "What the fuck?" The dark object was Alexei Braun.

"Well, he did just leave a freezing cold house," David said.

"Nobody should be walking around that cold. Because they should be dead."

"The sun is down. Does that affect things?"

Tyler banked and flew the drone towards a main thoroughfare. He zoomed in on a woman walking her dog and then turned on the thermal camera. Her head glowed like an orange light bulb and her body heat traced the contours of her clothes. Even the little dog was a blurry bundle of warmth bobbing at the end of its leash. "See? That's a person."

He zipped back to their street and followed Alexei Braun. "That's a snow man." He toggled from thermal to regular view and zoomed in.

"Uh...," David leaned back from his monitor, "is he looking at us?"

Alexei Braun's pale face filled their screens. His expression was blank, but there was something cruel in the slant of his cheek bones and dark narrow eyes.

"That's not possible. The drone is so high up he can't even hear it."

A sharp beep cried from the remote. David flinched.

"Battery is low," Tyler tapped his case, "But I have backups." He pivoted the drone to return to base.

The video feed fluttered and cut out. The remote lit up with another shrill tone.

Something smashed onto the pavement outside. It sounded expensive. Tyler jumped up. "What the fuck?!"

David looked at the last image frozen on the monitor. Buried behind the blocky glitches and bars was a dark blur. When he turned his head it looked like the feathers at the edge of a crow's wing, or the long sharp fingers of a blackened skeletal hand.

Tyler ran outside. David peered from the doorway. There was no sign of Alexei Braun.

Tyler brought the remains of his drone inside with a blistering tirade, cursing it for being a cheap piece of junk and then whining about how much he'd paid for it. "No wonder the thermal camera wasn't working. Where was the obstacle detection? The collision avoidance? I mean, there was still thirty percent left in the battery."

David felt awkward, as if it was his fault. He was reminded of a childhood friend who had once left with their broken toy and never played with him again. "Aw, that sucks, man. Wanna play some 'Call of Duty'?"

Tyler tossed the wreckage into the case and packed up. "N'ah, I'm gonna head out."

David opened up their favorite forum on his laptop. "We can...troll some camwhores?"

"Maybe later."

"Holy shit!"

Tyler turned back from the door. "What?"

The forums were blowing up with news about the Smokestack Killer. David skimmed the headlines. "Other police departments with disappearances and unsolved murders...searching abandoned smokestacks and finding bodies. More headless bodies!"

"Bullshit. Someone on the forum is just trolling. They're probably butthurt about all the attention you got."

"Where did you say my neighbor was from?"

"Ukraine, why?"

"It says the local police in Rovno, Ukraine are still pulling bodies from a smokestack. They estimate that there may be over fifty in total." He clicked a few links, and the same article appeared as the top item at the New York Times website.

Tyler moved a stack of old pizza boxes and sat down. "You think your neighbor is the Smokestack Killer?"

David chewed his fingernail and winced. "I think my neighbor is...a fucking vampire."

Tyler snorted. "You've been fappin' to Elvira for too long." He nodded towards a poster on the wall.

David glanced at the picture of the naked, ivory skinned woman arching her back and biting her full cherry lips with long white fangs. He normally fixated on her pendulous breasts, but at the moment all he could focus on was the dripping human heart clutched in her hands. "Just think about it! Blacked out windows, large basement, only comes out at night, pale, no body heat, um, Ukrainian..."

Tyler swiveled in his chair. "If you really wanna know, let's knock on that fancy door of his."

David stammered, afraid that if he didn't take the dare, Tyler might leave. "Um...me? G-go over there?"

"Not you. The cops."

"Oh. Is that safe?"

"Totally. No one will know we called them."

"I mean for the cops? If there's a vampire in there."

Tyler laughed. "We'll make sure they show up in full battle-rattle. Shields, helmets, body armor, machine guns, all that shit!"

He was talking about 'swatting', the most dangerous tool in the troll's arsenal. Tyler had sent SWAT teams to kick down the doors of his enemies many times. It was risky and extreme, but it might also be the best response to finding out there was a vampire next door. If David's theory was wrong, then perhaps Alexei Braun was just a normal, if somewhat prolific and particularly agile, serial killer.

"We should hold off until the sun comes up, just to be safe. We're okay in here. A vampire can't come into your home without an invitation."

Tyler shrugged. "But a serial killer can." It was not a comforting thought.

They played Call of Duty for a few hours, and then spent several more hanging out on forums and trolling different websites. David couldn't remember the last time he'd actually felt so happy, which was ironic considering that there was a murderous monster next door.

Tyler tried to salvage his drone's camera attachment. They wired it to the laptop and set it in the window in the hopes of getting another look at Alexei Braun. It was nearly dawn before they started to doze off. They had finished all the Mountain

Dew: Code Red in the fridge, and they could barely keep their bloodshot eyes open.

David sat in his gamer chair and rested his eyes. The thermal imagery on the large monitor washed over him, the warm blobs of color seeping through his closed eyelids like a nice relaxing lava lamp. A chill stirred him from his sleep, long dark fingers crawling across his eyes.

He jerked awake. Someone was walking up to the neighbor's house. It was impossible to tell who in the thermal imagery, but they glowed orange with body heat.

David prodded Tyler awake. He rubbed his eyes, squinted at the screen, and then adjusted something on the camera. The view switched to a low light image of Alexei Braun. The neighbor unlocked his front door and slipped inside.

They busted out laughing until they cried, loopy with sleep deprivation and relief. David slapped his greasy forehead. "I totally thought he was a vampire!"

Tyler giggled and scratched his neck beard. "I'm still swatting that fool."

David grinned and clicked back through the video. He magnified it to get a good clear image of Alexei standing in front of his house. "Welcome to the neighborhood, I guess."

He clicked back one frame too many, back to the thermal imagery. Alexei Braun's body was as warm as anyone...else.

"Tyler."

"Mmm?"

"You sure that camera works?" He rolled his cursor around the frozen image of Alexei Braun. His head, hands and legs all faded to purple, as cold and dead as the rocks that lined his driveway. The only thing warm with life was the contents of his stomach.

David and Tyler looked at each other, now very awake. They started working on their plan. First, they hopped on an unprotected Wi-Fi connection for a clean IP address. Next, they found the police scanner frequencies for the police department's Metropolitan Division. The 'Metro unit' was the city's real heavy hitter, responsible for tactical response and counter-terrorism. They downloaded the necessary keys to decrypt their radio communications so that they could listen to the raid in real time.

Finally, it was time to make the call. Tyler said, "You have to learn how to do it sooner or later."

David shrank in his chair. "I don't know what I should say. Do I use an accent? I don't know the Ukrainian accent."

"You're over thinking it, trust me. Nobody on the other end of that phone gives a shit. The second you say you're going to start shooting cops they will roll out."

David pulled on his headset and adjusted the microphone. His hands were shaking and his scraggly mustache prickled with sweat. He tried to remember all the swatting calls he'd listened to, especially those that Tyler had done.

He initiated the call.

"911, what's your emergency?"

"Uh...my name is Alexei Braun, um, I have hostages! If I see any cops I'm shooting first, you fuckin' got that?" He ripped off the headset.

Tyler gave him a slap on the shoulder and a proud nod. "There you go. You popped your cherry." He looked out the window and blinked at the morning glare. "Now it's show time."

They listened for the wail of approaching sirens to cut through the cheerful birdsong.

It was not show time. According to the chatter on the police scanners, it would not be show time for many hours. The Metro unit had been deployed to the airport in order to deal with a suspicious suitcase left at a terminal. When they finished with that they would have to get across the city, but all the freeways between here and there were jammed with rush hour traffic.

They tried to fight off their adrenaline crashes and stay awake. David microwaved some hot pockets while Tyler quizzed him on police codes. "Do you think I should call back?" David asked.

"Never call back. That's how they find you."

They eventually heard the bass rumble of a helicopter. The roof hummed as it churned the air overhead. "I would kill for another drone right now," Tyler huffed. They were exhausted but ready. They pulled on their headsets and listened to the decrypted police band radio.

The first vehicle to roar down their street was a huge black armored personnel carrier. It screeched to a halt in front of David's house. They had a front row seat to the action as eight SWAT team members poured out of the back of the vehicle, landed in a low crouch and continued in smooth combat glide positions until they were stacked up along either side of Alexei Braun's door. They were dressed in black from head-to-toe, with thick Kevlar vests, ballistic helmets, and even face masks. They bristled with belts of ammunition and high caliber weaponry.

David was in ecstasy. It was like Call of Duty in real life!

The SWAT team blasted the front door open with a breaching round from a shotgun and then tossed a flash-bang grenade inside. The wave of thunder rolled across the street and rattled David's window. The SWAT team swooped through the cloud of smoke and vanished.

David and Tyler listened to them move through the house. The officers didn't say much, but their voices were fluid and deep.

"Right clear."

"Left clear."

"All clear."

"Moving."

"Right clear."

"Left clear."

"All clear."

David's knee bounced like a jack hammer. Tyler scowled at him.

"Right clear."

"Left clear."

"GET ON THE GROUND! DOWN! DOWN!"

David and Tyler stared at each other, too tense to breath.

"Ten-fifteen." That was code for 'prisoner in custody'.

A voice bled into the radio. "*Ja ne rozumiju... ne rozumiju... Zalyšte mene u spokoji.*" It was some kind of Russian language, but the voice was mushy and frail. It sounded like the words of a toothless old man, not something that would come from Alexei Braun, even if he had just been body slammed by a SWAT team.

"Moving."

The SWAT team continued to sweep the rest of the house.

"Hold up. Got a basement here."

"Moving."

David and Tyler held their breath.

"Right clear."

"Left clear."

"All clear."

David shook his head. There was no way in hell they could have cleared that cavernous basement with a few quick glances.

Tyler whispered, "What?"

David fidgeted with the microphone on his headset. "I think they're missing something."

"Do they not sound professional to you? They got it under control."

David turned on his headset. Tyler grabbed his arm, but it was too late. "Um...," David had tried to lower his voice. It cracked immediately, "Look for a hidden door, or a trap door. Perverts have them in their dungeons, sometimes."

A deep voice growled, "Who is this? Clear the line."

Tyler punched him in the arm.

David cut his microphone and whined, "I'm sorry, I had to! There's something weird going on down there."

The radio crackled in their ears. "Got something."

An explosion rattled the speakers of their headsets.

David winced. "Damn...sounds like they breached an-other -"

"Contact!"

POP-POP-POP!

"Shots fired!"

The radios squealed and went dead. All of them.

David and Tyler slowly removed their headsets. A series of muffled explosions echoed inside the neighbor's house, barely audible over the thudding rotor of the police helicopter. Tyler slid the window open. The sporadic pops dwindled and stopped.

David pointed out the window with a trembling finger. Tyler looked frantically around the street. "What am I supposed to be looking at?"

"The sun. It looks like it's been down a couple minutes now."

The helicopter banked and flew away. They leaned out and watched its blinking tail rotor sail into the gathering darkness. David clutched his stomach. "What the fuck just happened? You've done this before, I mean, have you ever-"

Tyler ducked beneath the window and waved his arms. "Shut the fuck up!" The front door of the neighbor's house drifted open. A wisp of smoke rolled out into the cool night air.

David tugged his headset back on to eavesdrop on the Metro Unit.

"Ten-fifty-six. Standing by for a coroner."

David whispered, "What's a ten-fifty-six?"

Tyler looked confused. "Suicide, maybe?"

"The SWAT team is asking for a coroner."

Tyler looked green. "Oh shit. Who got shot?"

"I don't know! A cop? Alexei? Maybe that old Ukrainian dude?

The white coroner's truck arrived with an escort of two squad cars. Uniformed officers sealed off the neighbor's house with yellow crime scene tape and blocked the street with road flares.

Tyler peeked out the window. "They're going door to door!" He glared at David. "This is your fault!"

"Swatting him was your idea!"

"You told them about the basement! Now they're looking

for someone familiar with the house."

"Okay, um, but remember - vampires can't come in unless we invite them."

"What about fucking cops? With guns and dogs and shit?"

Knock-knock.

David and Tyler kept statue still and waited for them to go away.

An officer tapped the window with a flashlight. "Sir? I need you to answer your door."

David reluctantly opened the door a crack. He was shocked to find himself face-to-face with a female police officer. He immediately averted his eyes and started to sweat.

"Sir, did you witness anything that happened regarding the nearby incident this evening?"

"Oh, did something happen?"

Tyler shouted over David's shoulder. "You can't come in! You're not invited, we don't invite you!"

The officer checked her notepad. "David Burton?"

He gulped and his head jittered in the affirmative.

"Is this person your roommate?"

David looked back at Tyler. "He's my best, um, not my roommate. He's a friend."

She pushed the door open and beckoned Tyler. "Sir, I'm going to need you to step out here, please."

David's jaw dropped. "Wait, you can't. You're not invited!"

"If his name isn't on the lease, he can't stay," she insisted. "This area is on lock-down. I need your friend to come out, show me some I.D. and give a quick statement. Then he can be on his way."

Tyler slumped and took baby steps to the door.

The officer turned back towards David. "You don't have to cooperate now, we'll be back with a warrant." She glanced at the naked vampire on the wall and smiled. "Nice poster."

She led Tyler away. With each step he looked softer and weaker, until he was nothing but another obese, spineless man-child with a neckbeard.

David pointed the thermal camera up and down the street. The sputtering road flares were white hot distortions, but a scan of the SWAT team revealed that they were as icy purple as the neighbor's house. They huddled in a tight formation around someone with a violent white glow of his own. It was Alexei Braun. He had fed very well.

David uploaded all their footage from that night, along with a detailed account of everything that had happened. He begged for help, for both him and Tyler. He spread the truth about Alexei and the Smokestack Killings far and wide, along with urgent warnings of the vampire threat.

The response was instant and intense.

This soyboy has another Smokestack Theory. LOL.

Follow the money! *Smokestack* is a CIA front!

Fake news.

THE GREAT AMERICAN SCARE-OFF

"We've been searching the country to find the best undiscovered monsters and this week we're in Appalachia, a mysterious wilderness of logging camps, coal mines and dark hollers. Hundreds of hopeful haints, cryptids and creatures from the folk tales of Native Americans and Scotch-Irish immigrants have gathered from New York to Mississippi for their shot at fame and glory. In the end, our judges will select one winner to star in a brand new line of Halloween costumes and accessories."

A scaly green chupacabra in a swank suit lifted a microphone to his pearly smile. "I am your host, Ryan Chupacabra, broadcasting live from the Blue Hills of Virginia, and this is... The Great American Scare-Off!"

A crowd of monsters cheered for the camera, waving a confusing assortment of appendages.

"Let's meet our panel. Our first celebrity judge is none other than Bigfoot, the larger-than-life living legend. You've seen his blurry photos. You've heard about the size of his feet."

A giant ape-man smiled for the camera. "A lot of my ancestors live in Appalachia, so in a way, this is like coming home. I know the monsters here are ready for the national stage."

"Our second judge is The Mothman, Virginia's hometown hero who has gone on to terrify the world."

The Mothman rustled its black wings and stared with its round, glowing red eyes.

"And our final celebrity judge is rapper and fashion icon, Busta Rhymes."

Busta leaned into the camera. "I'm from Brooklyn, so I

need New York to represent. I want to see all y'all's baddest monsters!"

"Let's go backstage to check on our producer."

A woman dressed all in black except for an access badge and walkie-talkie stood before a group of monsters. "Unfortunately, we cannot see everybody at this time, so we will be making some preliminary cuts. If you are a fish with fur, I'm sorry. Halloween stores don't sell a lot of fish costumes."

A surprising number of dejected, hairy fish flopped towards the exit. The Snow-Snake paused and then reluctantly slithered after them.

She held up her hand. "Also, we've just received word from our sponsors that they can't promote any monsters that explode or self-destruct."

The towering Gumberoo and the coffin-shaped Terrashot lumbered out. The Squidgicum-Squee took a huge breath and then swallowed itself.

The producer checked her clipboard. "I'm also looking at you, Squonk."

A deformed creature, which appeared to be the combination of a blob fish and a warthog, wept piteously until it dissolved in its own bubbling tears.

Ryan Chupacabra waved to the camera. "It seems our judges have their work cut out for them. This first round of auditions is a harsh reality check for many of these aspiring monsters."

Bigfoot said, "I love Appalachia, its history, and its culture, but we are looking for mass appeal. If you're the type of monster that is only frightening to lumberjacks, please leave the stage."

The Axehandle Hound, Pickaliker, Splinter Cat, Log Gar and the large-nostriled Dungavenhooter slunk away.

Busta Rhymes said, "I ain't gonna front. Some of y'all monsters are doing they own thing, flipmode style, and that's cool. Upland Trout, you build your nest in trees. Goofus bird, you build your nest upside down. Gillygaloo, you lay square eggs.

Goofang, you swim backwards. I respect your style, but they ain't exactly, you know, 'scary'."

Bigfoot chimed in, "I see a lot of quote - unquote 'monsters' here that are barely even animals." He flipped through some index cards. "Hugag, you're a moose with legs so stiff you can't lay down. It also says here your lip is so big that you can't graze." He glanced at the next card. "Luferlang, will you come to the front, please?"

A rubbery, blue-striped horse scuttled like a crab to the edge of the stage. Its wide mouth was stacked with teeth.

Bigfoot squinted. "I hear that your bite is deadly…"

The Luferlang clacked its jaws. "It is certain death!"

Bigfoot continued, "But you only bite once a year? I hope for your sake that you bite on Halloween."

"Well, I usually do my bite around the middle of July."

Bigfoot tossed the card aside and scratched his leathery brow. "I need everyone's attention. If you do not, or cannot hurt people, please clear the stage."

There was a mass exodus of Appalachian monsters including the Sidehill Gouger, Teakettler, Hoopsnake, Wapaloosie, Swingdingle, Spurdoodle, Whiffenpoof and the Tote-Road Shagamaw.

"And if you're invisible," Bigfoot added, "you can't be made into a Halloween costume, so I don't know why you're even here. You may also leave. Or don't, I guess it doesn't matter."

The camera swiveled to the empty stage, where a few groans of disappointment could be heard.

Ryan Chupacabra looked solemn. "The field has been narrowed to only the deadliest and most visible contestants. We will return with our finalists in a moment."

A young production assistant in cargo shorts crouched beside the judge's table. Bigfoot quietly berated him.

"I don't care if they say they're my cousins. I want them out of my dressing room. Clear the whole greenroom if you have to."

The production assistant winced. "They just want a quick photo, and...I don't know how to get rid of them, they're boojums, wild men and woodboogers. They're all real big and mean-looking."

"And I'm not? Do it, or your career is over!" He pelted the teenager with a water bottle.

Ryan Chupacabra stood in front of a video wall strobing with lights.

"Welcome back to The Great American Scare-Off, sponsored by the Hallowmas Association. We go now to the stage, where our judges are deliberating about one of the dreaded Cherokee witches, the Raven Mocker."

A whirling ball of flames flew about the stage flapping its spindly arms like wings.

Bigfoot held up his hand. "That's good, thank you. Raven Mocker, you're a shape shifter, is that right?"

The ball of fire landed with a terrifying screech and transformed into a decrepit gray haired woman. She wore a deerskin poncho with a beaded panel and a pair of moccasins.

The judges leaned close to each other and whispered.

Busta Rhymes said, "Miss Raven Mocker, first off, I got to say much respect. You torment the sick and dying, you eat people's hearts and guts, and you steal their life force and add it to your own. That's real, and I know you been in the game since forever. Now, everybody knows you're a shape shifter, and that you can turn invisible, but you need to settle on a look. Nobody nowadays wants to wear a Halloween costume that has the name of the character printed on the front."

"Busta's right," Bigfoot said. "And to be honest, we can't use this native look you're wearing. If we sold that to everybody it would be too problematic. I'm afraid we're going to have to pass."

The Raven Mocker shrieked and shot off on a trail of flames.

"This is the moment you've been waiting for, America," Ryan Chupacabra said, "We're down to our final three contestants. Let's get to know them better. First up, we have a fearsome critter that is part bear, part panther, part lion and all 'Devil Cat'…it's the Glawackus!"

A shaggy animal prowled around on the stage.

"Next, this thirsty fiend is capable of draining a man's blood in a single gulp. The most feared monster of the swamp, the Gallinipper!"

A horrifying mosquito the size of a hawk hovered above the stage.

Busta Rhymes pumped his fist. "That's what I'm talking about right there. That's a straight up Dracula!"

"And our final contest tonight is a rare beast indeed. Hailing from the nightmares of Wisconsin's lumberjacks, this monster was born from the funeral pyre of a mistreated ox. It's the Hodag!"

A hulking frog-faced dinosaur with bull horns, a spiked back and a serpentine tail waddled into the spot light. It gouged the stage with its stubby clawed legs and roared.

The judges made notes and covered their microphones so that they could confer.

"I think these finalists are all strong contenders," Bigfoot announced. "But we have one more quality we'd like to see, and that is sex appeal. Adult costumes are the most rapidly growing sector of the market, so it is vital for monsters to showcase their sexiness."

Without warning the Mothman leapt into the air. He and the Gallinipper pursued each other across the flashing studio lights and slammed into one another.

Busta said, "I think Mothman just cast his vote!"

Bigfoot looked back to the stage. "Where's the Glawackus?"

The Hodag sucked down a black tail and smacked its rubbery lips.

Ryan Chupacabra blocked the view of the stage. "Well, there you have it. The Hodag is America's next Halloween costume! Look for Hodag merchandise everywhere official Hallowmas products are sold. Don't forget to stay tuned for the big giveaway. Up next, it's 'Are You Scarier than a Third Grader?'"

WORKING THE ROOTS OF PUMPKINS

Charlotte tied the little apron with the black rooster on it behind her daughter's back and then lifted her onto the stool by the kitchen counter.

"Are you ready to help your momma?"

Brianna clapped and cheered, "Pumpkin pie!"

Charlotte sprinkled flour onto a pastry board and unwrapped a ball of homemade dough. She handed her daughter a rolling pin. "Remember…"

"Not too thin, I remember." Brianna began to flatten the powdery mound into a circle.

Charlotte opened a wizened leather-bound book that also held a loose sheet of crinkled paper.

Her daughter lit up when she saw it. "Is this one of Gammy's recipes?"

"It's older than that. This was handed down by your great-great-great Gammy, although we do it a little differently these days." She preheated the oven and pulled out some baking sheets. "Great-great-great Gammy's name was Azuba. People thought she was a witch, but she was a priestess and a healer. She was very wise, and she worked Juju, Vodou, Hoodoo, Obeah, you name it."

Charlotte set a small orange sugar pumpkin in the sink and rinsed away the layers of garden soil. "There were a lot of people back then who didn't like Azuba. They were scared of what she could do and how she did it, so they threatened Azuba and her family."

Brianna stopped rolling the dough. "But she had magic, right? They couldn't hurt her?"

Her mother took out a long knife.

"Yes, Azuba had all kinds of magic. She could even bind her enemies by carving a root into a *poppet*."

"A puppet?"

"Something like that. It's what people now might call a 'voodoo doll', except these actually worked. When Azuba bound a body, they couldn't so much as lay a finger on her family. Of course, everyone believed in magic back then, so it wasn't hard for her enemies to get a mob together and drag her from her home."

She sliced the pumpkin in half and scooped out the seeds. She placed the empty halves on a foil lined sheet, drizzled them with oil and then slid them into the oven.

Brianna half-heartedly pushed the dough around with a gloomy look.

"Hey," Charlotte said, grabbing a handful of pulpy orange guts. "Should we roast up the seeds?"

"Can we make them spicy?"

"Of course." She rinsed the seeds and spread them evenly onto a sheet with paprika, Worcestershire sauce, Cajun spices and lots of salt. "Some of Azuba's family survived, and they passed down their knowledge through the generations. Unfortunately, her enemies had families too. They kept gathering power and authority as time went on."

The kitchen timer beeped.

"But over the years, people stopped believing that a little old lady could really do magic."

She lifted the thin circle of dough from the pastry board and gently unfolded it over a pie tin. She used the knife to trim the edges and then placed the tin in front of Brianna. "Ready?"

"Will you help me?"

Charlotte stood behind her and they both used their fingers to crimp the pie dough. "Like that, and that, and that." Brianna giggled and pinched the dough with her powdery fingers.

"Good job! Soon you'll be better than me."

"Baking is like magic, right?"

"I like to think of baking as more of a science." Charlotte slid the pie tin into the oven and retrieved the oiled halves of the sugar pumpkin. The rich nutty scent perfumed the air with warm autumnal memories.

Charlotte lined up a measuring cup and a pile of nested spoons. "Measurements, temperature, timing; everything's got to be just right."

She pricked a piece of pumpkin with a fork and it slipped through the skin.

"Just right," Brianna said.

"Do you remember your great-grandmother at all?"

Brianna squeezed her eyes real tight for a minute and then shook her head. "Not really."

"That's alright. You were pretty much a baby when you met her. Your great Gammy was one tough cookie. She figured out a new way to make poppets. Instead of using roots, she used gourds. All she needed was a pumpkin seed and a piece of someone's hair, a finger nail clipping, or something that touched their body. Anything she did to that pumpkin also happened to that person."

Charlotte peeled off the glistening orange skin and scooped out the steamy orange flesh. Brianna hovered near the food processor.

"Can I push the button?"

"You're in charge. I want you to blend it into a purée."

"Purée," Brianna repeated, committing the word to memory. She hit the button and watched the orange pulp churn and swirl inside the little chamber.

Charlotte pulled the roasted pumpkin seeds out to cool. She tossed some in a small bowl and pulled up a chair.

Brianna crunched on the seeds. "So what did Great Gammy do next?"

"Anything she wanted. She was a feared and respected conjure woman, but her family's old enemies were still out there, trying to make life hard. Well, they didn't know what hit them. At first they suffered terrible problems with their eyes and mouths. Doctors thought it was a rare disease or some unknown syndrome. It wasn't until they started dropping like flies that they started to understand. The doctors found out their insides were all mixed up, like they'd been scooped out with a spoon. The newspapers called it the work of 'Jack-o'-lantern the Ripper'."

"Did Great Gammy get away with it?"

"You don't remember that part either, do you?"

Brianna took a big handful of seeds and shook her head.

"Her enemies were working with the government men. They found her and kicked down her door, even though they didn't have any proof. Maybe she could have hired a lawyer, but like I said, she was one tough cookie. She lit a candle inside her newest pumpkin and the lead agent fell to his knees, puking up flames."

"Ewwww."

"Yeah, it was pretty bad. That's why my momma stopped us from messing with all that magic stuff. But that's okay." She brushed the pastry board and dabbed a spot of flour onto Brianna's nose. "Baking with you *is* a special kind of magic."

Brianna giggled.

The kitchen timer beeped again.

Charlotte took out the lightly baked pie crust. "Ready for the purée?"

Brianna raised her chubby arms and cheered, "Puréeee-eee!"

They mixed the pumpkin purée in a bowl with sweetened condensed milk and whisked in eggs, salt, ginger, cinnamon and nutmeg. They poured the smooth orange filling into the pie crust and then put it back in the oven. Charlotte closed the old leather book and tucked it away.

They danced and munched on pumpkin seeds while they cleaned up. Brianna offered to help with the dishes but then fell asleep on the couch instead. Charlotte tip-toed back to the kitchen and took the pie out before the final timer went off.

She cut herself a slice and watched the steam curl upward

like vines reaching for the sun. Charlotte put a dollop of fresh whipped cream on top and then took a bite.

She licked her lips, grabbed the sheet of paper from the old book, and crossed out the first name on the list.

THE YEAR WITHOUT A HALLOWEEN

(excerpt)

Chapter Eleven

"Halloween is canceled?!" Jim screamed at the top of his lungs. "That doesn't make any sense!"

Jim's dad spoke slowly to calm him down. "The snowstorm has covered the roads and none of the plows are ready. The mayor said tree branches are breaking under the weight of the snow. The power lines could get knocked down."

"You can't just cancel a holiday!" Jim stomped his foot. "Would they cancel Christmas for snow? I don't think so!"

Jim's mother rubbed his arms. "It's not safe out there, sweetie."

"We'll totally be careful. We already changed our costumes for the snow. We've got flashlights. We'll stay out of the street. Pleeeeeeease," Jim begged.

"Halloween is really just...postponed," his father said. "The mayor says they'll try to do something in two or three weeks."

"Three weeks? That's Thanksgiving! Are people going to hand out turkey?"

His mother shook her head. "We know tonight means a lot to you, but getting upset won't change anything."

"If you knew how much this night meant to me you'd be letting me go out *on-this-night*! Next year is a leap year! That means Halloween will be bumped to Sunday. That's *four years* of Halloween on school nights."

His father sighed. "Next year you'll be thirteen. That's a little old for trick-or-treating."

Jim's mouth fell open. He went to the basement and slammed the door.

"That could have gone better," his mother sighed.

Bryan, David and Eddie pretended that they'd missed the whole awkward meltdown.

Jim's father looked at them. "Would you boys mind calling your parents before the phone lines go down?"

* * *

Bryan slowly made his way down the basement stairs.

The stereo played a scratchy old record called the 'Chilling, Thrilling Sounds of the Haunted House'. Ghosts moaned while cats yowled at the moon.

Jim sat under the pool table wearing his favorite black cape and chewing on a pair of plastic fangs.

Bryan sat down next to him. "It sucks about the snow and everything. At least we can have all the candy our parents aren't giving out."

Jimmy took out the vampire teeth. "It's not about candy," he said. "Candy Club is about candy. We can hang out and talk about monsters anytime. Halloween is the one time of the year we get a break from stupid, boring normal life and everyone comes over to our side."

Bryan nodded. "It's the one day I get to be anyone other than me."

Jim's mother called down the stairs. "Sweetie?"

"What?"

She trotted down and smiled. "The other boys spoke to their parents. Everyone agreed it would be best if they stayed over-night until the roads are cleared. We'll make it a sleepover. You can stay up and watch scary movies."

"Really? They can stay over?"

"That's right."

Jim's face lit up. "It's going to be a full moon. Do you think we could do another round of sledding tonight?"

His mother put her hands on her hips. "I suppose, as long as you don't keep the neighbors awake. And be sure you stay away from the tree line. I'll leave the back porch-light on for you."

Jim ran and gave her a huge hug. "Thanks! Will you send David and Eddie down?"

"Sure thing." She gave him a peck on the top of the head. "Happy Halloween."

Jim watched her go, bouncing with excitement.

Bryan tilted his head. "Are you that pumped for more sledding?"

"I have something better in mind." He put the fangs back into his mouth and smiled.

#

The members of the Candy Club sat around their now empty bag. Even the wax lips had been opened.

"No way," David said. "You heard your parents, Halloween is canceled. Even the mayor said so! Besides, nobody is going to be handing out candy, so what's the point?"

Jim walked in a circle, eyes glittering with moonlight and snow. "There will be no other trick-or-treaters. Whoever answers their doors will give us all their candy. We just have to hit Heatherwood and we'll come back with more goodies than we've ever had in our lives!"

Bryan said. "But...won't we get in trouble?"

"My parents said we could go out. We're just going out a little farther. They want us to be safe and we will be. We're dressed for the weather. We don't even have to worry about cars."

"What about the people who answer their door? Won't

they call your folks?"

"We'll be disguised!"

Eddie looked out the basement window. "Not to be a total 'David', but it's starting to look like a blizzard."

David scoffed. "A 'total David'? What's that supposed to mean?"

"We won't be able to see where we're going," Eddie said.

"We grew up on this street," Jim laughed, "We could do this blindfolded."

"I don't live around here," David said. "What if I get separated from the group?"

"We're going down the hill. If you forget which way is down, check which way the snow is falling. It's impossible to get lost. Let's stop wasting Halloween and do this!"

❆ ❆ ❆

The boys had not seen the outside beyond the backyard that they'd mastered with sled trails and snow men. The rest of the world, it seemed, had been completely transformed. Summerhill Road was buried under several feet of snow, and only the gap between the trees gave any clue to where it lay. The stone walls that imposed order on the natural world had been swallowed. The dark tree line had been frosted white and made invisible. The light of the full moon, which should have illuminated the landscape, erased it with white glare.

Eddie's hockey mask and Bryan's bandages shielded their faces from the wind. Jim and David weren't so lucky. They wiped their runny noses on the backs of their gloves and the sleeves of their jackets. When those were covered in frozen stripes they wiped them on their fluttering candy bags.

Their silent footsteps filled instantly behind them. The biting wind snatched their breath before it fogged the air. It was like being in a fever dream; no footprints, no sound, no signs of breathing. It was eerie, and not in the fun haunted house kind of way.

"We are totally lost," David whined.

"We're fine. Downhill, remember?"

David stumbled and then pushed himself up, gasping for breath. "This feels as hard as going up and as slippery as going down."

Jim looked back the way they had come. He could still see the faint gray-squares of his garage doors. At least, he was pretty sure it was his garage. He looked for the light of his jack-o'-lantern, or any other pumpkins on his street. He saw nothing but snow blown sideways by the bitter wind.

There was not a single jack-o'lantern in the town to hold back the darkness of Halloween night.

Bryan recoiled in pain. "Aaahh!"

Jim helped steady him. "What happened?"

Bryan clutched his leg. "I don't know!" He brushed away the snow, confused by the object he couldn't see which he had discovered with his shin. It was rectangular with a round top.

Jim lifted his goggles and saw the block of white marble. "This is a gravestone."

A look around revealed headstones in all directions. "We must have crossed the street into the cemetery."

"The cemetery?" David shrieked.

The clouds parted and the moon hit the top of the hill like a spotlight. The shadow of a tree reached towards them and put an extra chill in their spines. It was a gnarled black tree with a deformed trunk that had been twisted around by centuries of wind. Its crooked limbs were draped in sickly vines and bloated with knots that wept tar-black sap.

A sudden surge of howling wind swirled around the cemetery gates, trapping the boys inside a blur of dead leaves and hissing ice.

"Look!" Jim pointed as the tree's spiral trunk crackled and began to unwind. It flexed and shivered like a tarantula breaking out of old skin. Its disjointed limbs snapped back into place like arm and finger bones. They rose up and then drove down into the soil. They dredged up mud-caked boxes and bundles wrapped in rotten shrouds. The branches ripped these apart and reverently held each treasure aloft; a bony hand that had been severed clean, a bundle of broken ribs, a leg bone bound in chains. The vines assembled these into a broken human husk, and with every rotation the tree reclaimed more pieces.

The boys turned to flee, but every path was veiled in blinding snow. The shrieking cyclone battered them and tore at their costumes, turning them back each time, forcing them to bear witness to the horror on the hill.

David covered his eyes.

Bryan clung to Jim. "What is it?"

Eddie screamed, "Who is it?"

The tree gently lowered its burden to the great stone slab. It was an unusually tall woman with tatters of black hair that hung over her face and down to her waist. Her long spindly arms and legs were covered in rusty chains, manacles and iron nails.

She slowly parted the tangled black curtain of hair.

❊ ❊ ❊

To be continued in 'The Year Without a Halloween'

PUMPKIN HEAD

Grady handed back the plastic tray of orange grease paint makeup and gestured to his face. "I'm more of a winter palette, but thanks."

"Don't be such a diva," Antoni said. "Besides, you'll look so cute."

Grady shook the bag with the tight green unitard. "I'll look like a kid in a production of Peter Pan."

Antoni hooked his thumbs into the straps of his overalls. "Do you want to go to this party with me or not?"

"Not. Was I being unclear? I want to stay in and watch a scary movie with you."

"I don't like scary movies."

Grady tossed the unitard onto his couch. "I've ended dates for less. What's so important about this party, anyway?"

"You said that you never kiss until after the third date. Going to a Halloween party in a couples costume has got to count for like ten dates."

"You're thinking of weddings, and I'm flattered, but a gentleman must have his standards."

"Come on, I never get to wear my overalls, and I found these really cute gardening gloves. If you're not going to let me kiss you tonight you could at least be my pumpkin."

Grady sighed and went into his bedroom. He returned in a sporty green tracksuit.

Antoni pushed up the brim of his straw hat. "That's the Halloween spirit!" He offered Grady the orange makeup again.

Grady grabbed a freshly carved jack-o'lantern from his window sill. "I'll use this instead."

Antoni gasped. "Oh my god, you're going to wear that on your head? Even better!"

"I was going to carry it."

"Oh please, you have to wear it!"

Grady held out the pumpkin. "Why not give me the overalls, and then you can wear this?"

Antoni recoiled. "Can't. I'm allergic to pumpkin."

"That's not a thing."

"It's true, I swear! Everything is covered in pumpkin spice this time of year, it's the worst. I can't even go into a Starbucks without sneezing my head off."

Grady tucked the pumpkin under his arm. "I'll go if I can carry it, but I'm not wearing a slimy pumpkin on my head."

"Next time I'll grow a more obedient pumpkin."

"You'll be lucky if there is a next time. Now, who's going to be the designated driver?"

After much debate, they agreed to pay the surge pricing and took an Uber.

They arrived at an imposing Tuscan style mansion with thick medieval walls built directly into the hillside. The house was cradled in dark rock and crowned with sighing red leaves.

Antoni took Grady by the hand and pulled him towards the throbbing music. A few small clusters of people were visible through the murk, leaning among the pillars or standing on the cold tile with sushi and canapés.

"I'm going to go amuse my '*bouche*'," Antoni shouted. "Find us some drinks?"

Grady wandered through the largely empty space. The echo of concussive bass made him slightly nauseous.

A guy with slick dark hair, a white dress shirt and an exposed superman logo tee-shirt squinted at him. "Dude, what are you supposed to be? A basketball player?"

"I'm a pumpkin." Grady lifted the jack-o'lantern. "What are you supposed to be?"

The guy moved his red tie aside and pulled at the open edges of his shirt, wrinkling the fake muscle suit underneath.

'I'm Superman, bro."

"Shouldn't you be wearing Clark Kent glasses?"

"Chicks don't dig glasses." He checked his watch. "This party's dead. I'm out."

Grady sighed and headed to a bar station manned by a svelte tattooed hipster in a green silk vest. He shook up a cocktail and asked, "What can I get you, boss?" His face was airbrushed orange and yellow with a perfect jack-o'lantern paint job that somehow blended seamlessly with his well-groomed beard.

Someone bumped into Grady from behind. He turned and saw a short man in a swollen pumpkin costume waddling past.

Grady asked, "Can I get a different costume?"

The bartender shook his head.

Grady headed outside. The night air was cold, but it was warmer than the mansion. He wondered if that was because it was built into the hillside. The whisper of leaves drew his attention upward. Darkness had stolen the warm colors and bound the swaying trees, stony hill and mansion into one ink-black mass that loomed over him.

He shivered and took out his house key. He used it to punch a series of holes around the bottom of the pumpkin and then ripped it out. He took a deep breath and put the jack-o'lantern over his head.

It was a little clammy, but he'd done a good job of cleaning out the guts and seeds when he'd carved it. It even smelled kind of nice.

He went back inside and was relieved by the reduction of pounding bass. Either his pumpkin shell muffled the noise or the sudden influx of people were absorbing it. The party was now in full swing.

He searched for Antoni and found him in a corner, eating sushi and staring into the eyes of a broad shouldered man in a skimpy Tarzan costume.

Antoni noticed Grady and ran over with a wide-eyed smile. "You actually did it! You're the best!"

We Bleed Orange & Black

Grady's pinched expression was lost inside his pumpkin helmet.

"Sorry," Antoni said, "I thought this party would be a little livelier."

Grady pulled off the pumpkin. The bass flooded back in, rattling his skull. "That guy in the loincloth seemed pretty lively."

Antoni gasped and looked around. "Loincloth? Where?"

Grady tried to point him out, but he was gone. "I didn't agree to come here just to watch you flirt with other guys."

"I'm here with you. The couples costume was supposed to show that."

Grady felt a scream rising in his throat, but Antoni was genuinely being sweet. He put the pumpkin back on to hide his burning ears.

Antoni rubbed Grady's chest. "You're so dramatic. I bet you were Goth AF in high school."

Grady shook his pumpkin head and looked away.

"Come on, admit it," Antoni said, poking him in the stomach. "You used to hang outside the drama club in your eye-liner, smoking little clove cigarettes."

"Seems like someone's been stalking me on Facebook."

Antoni shrugged. "Who doesn't love a good throwback Thursday?"

"Well, if you can't handle me at my Goth AF, you don't deserve me at my pumpkin AF."

Antoni laughed. "We need to dance, but first we need those drinks. Here, finish this." He used his chopsticks to poke the last piece of sushi into the jack-o'lantern's mouth. He put his arm around Grady. "Speaking of Facebook." He held out his phone and took a few selfies. Grady tried not to blink but each flash went straight into his eyes.

He heard Antoni say, "I heard that instead of a wine cellar, they have a wine cave!"

When the green blur faded, he was gone.

Grady walked around the bustling party, stomach alternately fluttering and roiling. He couldn't wait for Antoni to come back so that he could throw his arms around him, but he'd been burned by boys like him before. It was hard to tell with the costumes and strobing lights, but he could have sworn that he saw a dozen of Antoni's ex-boyfriends around the dance floor. He'd been doing some Facebook stalking of his own.

A short sob turned his head.

A girl in a red wig and sparkly mermaid dress covered her mouth and quickly walked away from a stoic prince. Behind him, a guy and girl dressed as mustard and ketchup bottles argued in terse whispers. Little islands of strife formed across the dance floor while single people along the walls drowned their loneliness in red solo cups.

Grady went looking for the wine cave.

He found a grand, roughhewn staircase that spiraled down into darkness. It was ridiculously ostentatious, yet there was also something somber about the primitive passage. Either way, he was convinced that he did not belong there. He descended in a series of quiet pauses.

He reached the bottom and peeked around a rock wall. It was a gloomy subterranean chamber and its far wall was dominated by a crude archway of oblong boulders capped by a colossal slab. Suspended from the craggy arch, in perfect contrast, was a diaphanous curtain that rippled in the stagnant air like mercury.

Grady barely registered any of it. He was fixated on the tall Tarzan who was leading Antony through the veil.

He sprinted back up the steps, self-immolating with white-hot humiliation. A dozen of Antoni's ex-boyfriends were waiting at the top, smirking in triumph.

"You can have him," Grady shouted. "And give him this!" He plucked off the pumpkin, but before he could smash it at their feet they all disappeared. He flinched and looked around the party. Other than the bickering couples and crestfallen singles, the place was suddenly empty.

He slowly nestled his head back inside the jack-o'lantern.

The ex-boyfriends reappeared, laughing as they beckoned him down the stairs. The dance floor refilled with men and women casting sultry glances and instigating fights between couples.

He hurried back into the chamber below. The ex-boyfriends parted to let him approach the billowing veil.

He reached out to part the gossamer layers and his fingertips went blissfully numb. The rest of his body ached in comparison. All those lonely years he'd spent swallowing tears had left him brittle. He was too frail to carry his broken heart one more step.

But the veil was as soft as a baby blanket. It fluttered like a lover's eyelashes. It radiated all the warmth and safety of a shared bed.

And beyond the veil, there was peace.

He stepped through the shimmering membrane and felt the embrace of the dead gray void.

His jack-o'lantern head collided against the veil. It spat him back into the chamber.

"Antoni!"

He'd caught a glimpse of Antoni trapped on the other side, as still and transparent as a fossil. Grady pulled off the pumpkin to make another run at the veil, but it was gone. There was nothing behind the archway but a blank stone wall.

"Hold on, Antoni! I'll save you!"

Grady hustled back up the stairs one more time. The phantom party goers watched him with naked amusement. He ran over to the bartender.

The hipster raised one orange eyebrow.

Grady huffed, "Jack-o'lanterns...they're supposed to ward off spirits, right?"

The bartender nodded. "Yeah, I think that's how it works, once you put a candle in them."

"Great! Are there any pumpkins or candles around here?"

"I know for a fact there aren't. The owner was very specific about that when he hired us."

"Damn it!" Grady paced and tried to chew his nails, touching the cold wet mouth of his pumpkin. "Hey...do you have a cigarette?"

The bartender took a pack from inside his green vest. "I only have cloves."

Grady reached out and took a slim brown cigarette. He stuck it through his jack-o'lantern grin and leaned in for a light. He tasted the familiar cloying smoke and turned around.

The pulsing glow of his pumpkin head fell onto the sneering spectral revelers. They shrieked and crumbled into pitch-black clumps that scattered into the shadows like cockroaches.

Grady delved back into the earth. The gang of ex-boyfriends withered beneath his glare. The jack-o'lantern's light peeled away their masks of stolen memories and revealed the hollow, jealous spirits beneath. They decomposed as they fled back through the veil.

Grady went after them. The veil quivered and retreated from his presence, warping inward like a distending soap bubble. He marched through the tunnel, forcing it back until he reached Antoni.

He wrapped his arms around him and pulled him from the abyss. The substance and warmth returned to Antoni's body. Grady carried him through the great stone archway, up the stairs and back to the world of the living.

Antoni opened his eyes and gazed up in awe. Grady's jack-o'lantern head blazed against the night sky and his mouth trailed vapors that wreathed him in a swirling nimbus.

Grady lowered him to the damp grass, knelt down, and removed the pumpkin.

"I'm...alive," Antoni said. "You saved me, didn't you?"

Grady smiled. "I think that counts for at least three dates."

He leaned down and gave Antoni a long, deep kiss.

Their lips parted, and Antoni sneezed in Grady's face.

"Sorry!" He sniffled. "I'm allergic to pumpkin."

Epilogue

HOW TO PRESERVE YOUR PUMPKIN

And just like that, it was November.

Ben took down the giant spiders in the morning, like he had promised. He tried to gather all the fake webs from the porch railing but the more he pulled, the longer they got. He took his time, walking back and forth, swimming through spider webs and enjoying the crunch of red and orange leaves beneath his feet. Yesterday's costume was already in the trash. All that remained was the pumpkin grinning on the front step.

His family had bought different stencils and fancy carving tools for their own pumpkins, but Ben always went with the same classic design; two right-side up triangle eyes, a smaller one for the nose, and a broad, cheerful smile of alternating square teeth. He even went out of his way to select the same sized pumpkin – just wider than a basketball. Each year Ben grew taller, his costumes changed, but the friendly face of his jack-o'lantern stayed the same.

He looked at the stains where his family's pumpkins had been. They'd been intricately carved yet barely hollowed out. Their wet stringy guts and fistfuls of seeds had rotted, transforming them overnight into black cauldrons of mold. Ben's well-manicured pumpkin was the only one left.

Ben sat down next to it and let out a long sigh.

"You know," the jack-o'lantern said, "Some people celebrate 'The Day of the Dead' until November second."

"Nobody around here. Halloween is over."

Ben shoved his hands into his pockets and stood up. The pumpkin smiled. Its gap toothed mouth and eyes were still rimmed in gold, even without the candle light. It was clean and fresh. The air was cool and dry. It would keep for a while.

A few days later, Ben was back on the porch with a spray bottle. He sprayed the pumpkin inside and out.

"That tickles!" the jack-o'lantern giggled.

"It's bleach and water. It's supposed to keep you clean."

"You've never done this before."

Ben gave it a final spritz. "I convinced my folks that pumpkins and corn are fall harvest decorations, not just for October. I think you should be able to hangout through Thanksgiving at least. They agreed that you can stay, but only until the first sign of rot."

"Won't be long. Tis the season, you know."

"Ha ha."

"I wasn't joking."

"Good, because it wasn't funny." Ben stomped inside.

The following week Ben hunched down on the porch with a bowl of soapy water and gave the pumpkin a bath.

"This smells nicer than the bleach," the jack-o'lantern said.

"It's peppermint. It's supposed to be a natural antifungal or something." Ben frowned. "Why isn't it working?"

"It's working great! You don't see any other exposed, chopped up veggies out here smiling, do you?" The pumpkin's mouth and eyes had lost their luster. Wrinkles puckered at their corners. A shadow stained the inside of the shell, growing darker every day.

"If my parents see this I'll have to get rid of you. Don't you even care?"

"I care that we had an awesome Halloween. I got to see lots of cute kids in costumes, and I even scared away an evil spirit! It had beady little eyes and a spooky white skull for a face. Oh, you know what? That may have been a possum."

"So what, it's over now? It doesn't matter what I want?"

"Ben, what's wrong? You were in such a good mood all October."

The boy dried his hands on his pants and sat on the step.

He fished a cellophane roll of Smarties from his coat pocket, unwrapped it, shook out a few, and then carefully closed it back up. He crunched quietly to himself for a moment.

"I'm too old to go trick-or-treating anymore," he said.

"Is that true?"

"That's what they tell me."

"Your parents?"

"My friends." Ben stood and paced. The leaves underfoot had become a soggy brown carpet. "They said they don't want to go anymore. I was complaining about it to my parents, and they listened, but...I could tell they thought so, too."

"There's more to Halloween than trick-or-treating. You love carving pumpkins, decorating, scary movies, all of it."

"You don't get it. You grew up in a pumpkin patch, and then you became a jack-o'lantern. Your whole life is Halloween!" Ben kicked at the wet leaves. "The same people who decide I'm too old to trick-or-treat are the same ones that decide it's too early to get excited, when it's too early to decorate, and when the decorations have to come down. It's not fair! They get to enjoy the rest of the stupid year. I get a few weeks in the fall and...I only get one night where I fit in. Now they've decided to take that from me, too."

The jack-o'lantern's teeth had curled and its mouth had narrowed. Still, it offered him a shy smile.

"Ben, I'm glad you chose me from the pumpkin patch. I really liked it here. We had such a great October! You gave me my face, and I made it through Halloween night without getting knocked down and smashed! I never thought I'd get to see this much of November. You were right, I am a harvest decoration. If you go back to my patch, you'll see that it's been harvested and cleared along with the fields of wheat and corn. At some point you have to lay things to rest. Nothing lasts forever."

Ben looked away and wiped his cheeks.

"Oh yeah? Well, you're stuck here with me. I get to decide when it's over." He went inside and slammed the door.

The autumn air had been crisp like cider, but the November rain was metallic and cold. Even when it let up the ground never quite dried out. The sun was too weak, barely able to keep its pale bald crown above the dim horizon. Ben had towel-dried the pumpkin to keep it from getting too wet, dabbed it with Vaseline to keep it from drying out, sealed all its edges with hair spray and scraped layer after layer of mold from the inside of its thinning shell. None of it had helped for long.

Now he shivered on the porch, carefully using a paint-brush to coat the pumpkin with a can of shellac. It was the last thing he could think of, and it actually seemed to be working. The jack-o'lantern glistened with a healthy amber glaze. Ben breathed into his hands to warm them and then rubbed his red ears and nose.

"I think this is it. This is the fix!"

The jack-o'lantern said nothing.

Ben searched its dark sunken eyes. "Hello?"

He gently touched the pumpkin's stem. A crack split from its eye to its nose.

"No no no," He cradled the jack-o'lantern to hold it together. Its face caved in. The shell liquefied and poured through his fingers.

A hot tear slipped down Ben's frozen cheek. He bit his chapped lip and carried the runny handfuls of pumpkin to the trash can.

His boots crunched across the frosted skeletons of leaves. There was nothing on the horizon but bare black trees and end-less waves of gloomy clouds. He shook off his numb wet hands and trudged inside.

He stopped on the top step. Nestled inside the black re-mains of the pumpkin lay a single pale seed. He hadn't hollowed it out as well as he'd thought.

What had the jack-o'lantern said? *Nothing lasts forever*.

Ben picked out the seed and held it tight. No matter how dull or dark the rest of the year may be, he could always be able to look forward to October. He would return to the pumpkin patch to find his old friend, and they would smile.

ABOUT THE AUTHOR

Jeff C. Carter's stories have been featured in dozens of anthologies, translated for international markets and adapted for podcasts. He lives in Los Angeles with a cat, a dog, and a human.

His hobbies are legion, including but not limited to: making props and costumes, special FX makeup, Japanese art, calligraphy and language, climbing, surfing, travel, escape rooms and survival skills. His favorite sport, holiday and religion are ALL Hallowe'en.

You can find more of his work at Jeffccarter.com

If you enjoyed this book, please leave a review. Thanks!

BETWEEN THE TEETH

collects 16 tales of horror and science fiction that will sink their fangs into you and not let go.

- A serial killer ends up in an emergency room, but a heart attack may be the least of his problems.

- A researcher hunts a rare spider in the jungles of Myanmar.

- A greedy dentist gets the most interesting client of his life.

Witness soldiers trapped in a crocodile infested swamp, a preacher hunting demon outlaws, and karma catching up to a Bangkok body snatcher. Whatever flavor of the macabre you crave, you will find it Between the Teeth.

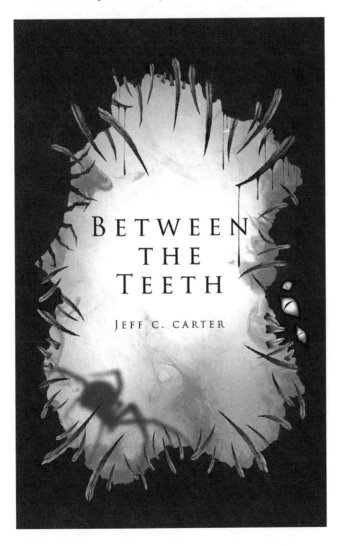

CRITERION
is the world's mightiest hero.
His sidekicks just found his body.

Shattered by the death of their idol, the Cadets are consumed with strife and jealousy. The only thing keeping them together is terror.

What hope do they have against an enemy that can kill anyone?

Who killed Criterion? Who will die next?

CRITERION is available in print and e-book at this link.

To get the first 10 chapters free, news and more giveaways sign up for the newsletter.

Made in the USA
Middletown, DE
27 October 2020